ROBERT SWINDELLS

Blackout

D1079855

OXFORD
UNIVERSITY PRESS

OXFORD
UNIVERSITY PRESS

Great Clarendon Street, Oxford OX2 6DP

Oxford University Press is a department of the University of Oxford.
It furthers the University's objective of excellence in research, scholarship,
and education by publishing worldwide in

Oxford   New York

Auckland   Cape Town   Dar es Salaam   Hong Kong   Karachi
Kuala Lumpur   Madrid   Melbourne   Mexico City   Nairobi
New Delhi   Shanghai   Taipei   Toronto

With offices in

Argentina   Austria   Brazil   Chile   Czech Republic   France   Greece
Guatemala   Hungary   Italy   Japan   Poland   Portugal   Singapore
South Korea   Switzerland   Thailand   Turkey   Ukraine   Vietnam

Oxford is a registered trade mark of Oxford University Press
in the UK and in certain other countries

British Library Cataloguing in Publication Data

Data available

ISBN: 978-0-19-912937-9

3 5 7 9 10 8 6 4 2

Printed in China by Printplus

Paper used in the production of this book is a natural,
recyclable product made from wood grown in sustainable forests.
The manufacturing process conforms to the environmental
regulations of the country of origin.

The author is grateful to Ms Dyddgu Pritchard Owens, who was kind enough to assure him that the word Golfodd, the name of the town in this novel, is 'easy on the ear'.

ONE

If There's a War

The props were old and rotten. Mary Swaine shivered, imagining the whole weight of Ling Hill pressing down on them. She was always nervous when they played in the mine, but she kept it from the others. If you're in a gang you do what the gang does. If you don't, you're out.

There was light ahead. The four children walked towards it up the shallow slope. Each step she took made Mary feel better. Caving sounds exciting when people talk about it, but it's not much fun when you're actually underground.

1

I bet a war's like that as well, she thought; *thrilling to talk about, horrid if you're in it.*

It seemed war was coming. People talked about nothing else lately. This was the last weekend of the summer holidays. The gang ought to be dreading the start of school the day after tomorrow, but they weren't. There was a feeling in the air – a sense of something coming that would sweep away routine in favour of the unexpected. People wore solemn expressions discussing the probability of war, but underneath they were excited. You could tell.

'All I hope,' said Tom as the gang emerged into sunlight, 'is that if there's a war it lasts till I'm old enough. Rotten luck if it's over in a year or so.' Tom was Mary's twin.

They looked alike, but weren't. For one thing, Tom seemed quite happy in the old mine. Mary was fond of her brother but she envied him that. She wished he wasn't so keen on this war everybody seemed so excited about. She looked at him. 'You're twelve,' she said. 'If it started today, it'd have to last at least six years for you to get into it, and it won't.'

'Why shouldn't it?' Tom demanded. 'There was

a hundred years war once, we done it in history.'

'Hundred *years*?' Dil laughed. 'Soldiers must've been doddering by the time *that* was over, isn't it?'

Gary shook his head. 'Don't want no part of it myself anyhow. My grandad was in the trenches in the Great War, see, and you know what he got: a permanent limp and a night watchman's job at the boring old museum. *Nothing glorious about war*, he tells me when I asks him what it was like. *Nothing but mud and lice and losing your mates.* Ner.' He shook his head again. 'You can keep it for me.'

'Yes, but you'd do your bit if it came to it,' insisted Tom. 'I know you would.'

Gary shrugged. 'Know more'n *I* do, then.' He grinned. 'I'd go live in the mine, they'd never find me there.'

'Yeah,' said Dil. 'You could dig for gold, like your ancestors did.'

'I wouldn't find any,' he growled. 'Only gold in Golfodd's in the museum. My great-grandad worked like a slave for twenty years and found half a cupful, or so my grandad says. Listen.' He looked at his three friends. 'If anybody asks, we've been messing about on the hill. Don't mention the mine, or they'll never let us out of their sight again.'

At the foot of the hill the footpath forked and the gang split up. It was twenty minutes to four on Saturday the second of September, 1939. It was the last day of peace, though nobody knew that then.

TWO

The Old Cogs

Dil walked home slowly, making it last. Not much fun to be had at home, what with Dad being Councillor Tenby and Mam being his door-mat. Dil was their only child, they'd almost given up hope when Mam became pregnant, and they'd worried about her every day since. Parents do worry, of course, only natural, but the Tenbys took it to extremes. Especially Dad. Dil thought if he had his way, she'd be in a glass case in the museum, next to the gold coins.

He was on the doorstep when she opened the garden gate. *Been there half an hour, I suppose,* she thought. *Ten to four in the afternoon, second of September, broad daylight, and he's on pins as if it were midnight in the middle of winter.*

'Hello, Dad,' she said, walking up the path between borders of lupin and red-hot poker. 'Breath of fresh air, is it?'

The councillor shook his head. 'Not really, Dil, no. Your mother and I wondered what you were up to, you were gone so long.' He sidestepped so she could enter.

'Wasn't up to nothing,' said Dil, brushing past him. 'Playing on the hill, that's all.'

'*Anything,*' corrected her father. 'You weren't up to *anything*, Dilys. *Weren't up to nothing*'s a double negative. Who was with you?' He followed her along the hallway, watched her drape her blazer over the newel post.

Dil sighed. 'Mary and Tom Swaine, Gary Mossman.' She knew what was coming.

'Swaines're all right, but I never did like that Mossman boy. Don't trust him. His father ran off with some floozie and he'll do the same himself someday.' He eyed his daughter. 'Didn't take you anywhere near the old mine, did he?'

'Why should he?' snapped Dil. She avoided

6

answering the question yes or no, because she hated lying to her parents, though her dad's wittering would make a saint lie.

'Why *should* he?' echoed the councillor. 'Perhaps because Mossmans *dug* that mine, Dilys. It belongs to the Mossman family, who ought to have filled it in years ago as a danger to children. Instead, they stuck up a notice with a skull and crossbones and the word DANGER, as if *that*'s going to keep kids from exploring. Cheap, see, a notice. Cheaper than paying a firm to fill it in. And that's what I mean about the Mossmans: you can't trust 'em.'

Dilys was just wondering if she dared stick up for Gary when her mother called from the kitchen. 'Ivor, Dilys – tea's ready.' She followed her father to the dining room, where the table was set with scones and jam, and tea in the big brown pot.

They took their places. Dil's mam filled her dad's cup and passed him the milk jug. 'D'you think we really *will* have to go to war, Ivor?' she asked quietly.

The councillor snorted. 'How would *I* know, Annie?' he growled. 'I'm a Golfodd town councillor, not God.'

'Sorry, dear,' murmured Annie. 'I was making conversation, that's all.'

Dil stared at her plate, wishing Mam would stick up for herself. *There's a surprise, Dad, isn't it*, said a little voice inside her head. *You admitting you're not God, and me and Mam thinking all this time that you were.* She wished she dared say it out loud.

'I've no time for small talk at the moment,' said the man who wasn't God, smearing jam on half a scone. 'Got to think, see. Big meeting Monday, full council. Vital matters to resolve. Confidential, or I'd tell you.' He glanced at Dil. 'Fill my cup again, will you, Dilys? Got to keep the old cogs oiled, isn't it?'

Dil leaned across and poured. *The old cogs can rust away for all I care*, she thought, but all she said was: 'There you are, Dad.' *Hey*, hissed the rebellious voice in her head, *what if war comes and Dad's posted to some faraway place; won't that be absolutely wizard?*

Yes, but it won't happen will it? He's thirty-three, too old for the Army. And besides, Golfodd would fall apart with him gone. If you don't believe me, ask him.

THREE

Praying for Peace

The morning sun shone down on Ty Coch, Golfodd's only inn. Tom Swaine rolled out of bed in his room above the bar and pulled back the curtain. The south slope of Ling Hill lay bathed in warm light which dazzled on the whitewashed walls of Ling Hill Farm. It was a tempting scene, all the more tempting because today was Sunday and tomorrow was school.

Flipping chapel, thought Tom. Golfodd Bethesda chapel was a short walk away on High Street South. It was where the family Swaine spent most of each Sunday morning, rain or shine, listening to Old Testament stories which

9

Reverend Pike sometimes edited to make them fit his themes. There were sermons too; long ones. Reverend Pike was famous for the length of his sermons. *Why can't we drop it, or go to church instead?* wondered Tom. Saint David's church was right opposite the inn, on the other side of East Road on the corner with the High Street. The vicar preached sermons too, but he kept them short and to the point. The Tenbys were church people, and Dil was always free at least half an hour before Reverend Pike's flock emerged blinking into the light.

Sunday breakfast was a simple affair: Tom's mother usually had guests to see to before chapel. The family had porridge and tea, and then the four Swaines were on the street in their Sunday clothes, walking to Bethesda.

'Morning, Kenneth,' greeted those they passed along the way. Everybody knew the land-lord of Ty Coch, which in English means Coach House. What they *didn't* know was why Libby Swaine, brought up strict Methodist, had married a man who kept a pub.

Reverend Pike's theme that morning, to nobody's surprise, was Peace. The Israelites, he said, flattened the walls of Jericho with music, not artillery. Daniel did not storm the lions' den with tommy-guns, but with faith. As for the Egyptians, they were overcome by frogs and flies, not heavy bombers and poison gas. Tom pictured an army of frogs advancing on Berlin under squadrons of flies. He hadn't meant to: the picture formed by itself and he nearly laughed out loud. He managed to stop himself, which was lucky: it wouldn't have been a good idea to laugh in chapel.

Winding up the proceedings, Reverend Pike prayed for peace. 'Guide Thou the footsteps of the politicians in the ways of peace,' he intoned, 'and confound the aggressors, the lovers of war, even as Thou didst confound the giant Philistine Goliath, so that he did fall to little David.'

Walking home, Tom said, 'D'you think the Germans prayed for peace this morning, Dad?'

His father nodded. 'Bound to have, I suppose, son.'

'And they have the same God as us, don't they?'

'Of course. Nonconformism began in Germany.'

11

'So it'll be all right, won't it?'

The landlord shook his head. 'You'd think so, Tom, but it's not always as straightforward as that.'

'If war comes after all that praying,' put in Mary, 'how can we go on believing that God listens?'

Her father frowned at her. 'Thou shalt not tempt the Lord thy God,' he said, in such menacing tones that neither twin pursued the matter, but two minutes later a neighbour came to his garden gate to tell them he'd just heard on the wireless that Britain was at war with Germany.

FOUR

These Things Shall Be

The school year began with assembly, attended by everybody. School years always did, but this time it felt different. It was the first full day of war. Any minute, German aeroplanes could appear and start dropping bombs, spraying deadly gas, disgorging paratroops. There was a buzz of excitement in the packed hall: excitement that was half frightening, half delicious.

The head didn't appear straightaway, and Tom Swaine slipped into a fantasy. A machine gun had been set up on the roof: the sort of gun that has a ridged barrel and a belt of ammunition that comes looping out of a box. The sky was black with Nazi planes, and Tom had volunteered to take the place of the dead gunner. A plane came swooping in, machine guns chattering. Golfodd School had a strategic importance, Hitler had ordered its destruction at all costs. Ignoring the bullets that pinged all around him, Tom got the plane in his sights. He didn't just start blazing away, but waited coolly till the machine was practically on top of him before giving it a short, accurate burst. Bits flew off the fuselage and the plane banked away, smoke pouring from its engine. As teachers and pupils watched from the playground, it failed to clear Ling Hill and crashed in a fireball near the farm.

Everybody was cheering and waving at Tom, but he hadn't time to wave back. Already, another plane was approaching in a shallow dive, bombs under its wings. With a grin and a wink at those below, he swung the machine gun into position and waited for the aircraft to come within range.

'What on *earth* do you think you're playing at, Thomas Swaine?'

Tom's fantasy disintegrated instantly and he realized he'd been swivelling about, making machine-gun noises with his mouth. The head was glaring at him from the platform. Kids were sniggering. His cheeks felt hot.

'N ... nothing, sir,' he stammered. 'Sorry, I was just...' *No good saying I was defending the school, is it?* 'Clearing my throat, sir.'

'I'll clear your throat for you, laddie,' growled the head, 'if you ever make another racket like that in my assembly. Stand up straight for goodness sake, and take your hands away from your face so we can see you've the grace to blush.'

The head nodded to Miss Owen, the piano tinkled. The hymn was 'These Things Shall Be'. Tom croaked the words, feeling a total idiot. At least his face was cooling. After a short prayer, the head spoke at length to the pupils about some changes they might expect, now that war had been declared. Council workmen would be coming to put up an air-raid shelter in the yard. Miss Owen's needlework classes would start straightaway sewing blackout curtains for every window in the school. From tomorrow, all pupils should carry their gas masks to school every day. As a small town in the country, Golfodd would expect evacuee children to arrive sooner or later

15

from the cities, to stay with families till the bombing was over. These children would be enrolled at Golfodd School and should be made welcome, because they were bound to feel homesick. Many fathers would be called up into the armed forces, and this would be upsetting for mothers and children alike. Therefore they would all have to make a special effort to be kind and gentle towards one another in the troubled times ahead.

There was no mention of anybody coming to install a machine gun on the roof. Still, you can't have everything, and Tom suspected the war might provide the gang with activities that'd make exploring the old mine seem pretty tame.

FIVE

Zeppelins

Dil's dad bounded up the town hall steps at five to seven. He was fit, and liked to show it. He also liked to be punctual. The meeting was supposed to kick off at seven on the dot, but when Councillor Tenby strode into the council chamber it was empty.

Typical, he fumed. *Biggest crisis since 1914 and they can't be bothered turning up on time. Good job the town's got me, that's all I can say.* He threw himself into a chair and sulked, watching the door.

The last man came panting through it at

twenty-five past. Councillor Ramsay gasped his apology and took his place. 'I've been giving Gwen a hand with the blackouts,' he explained. 'In case they send zeppelins over tonight.'

'*Zeppelins?*' scoffed Ivor Tenby. 'Zeppelins went extinct more than twenty years ago, Councillor. They've got heavier-than-air machines now, otherwise known as aeroplanes.' He hoped this might get a laugh, but it didn't. Only Ivor Tenby was ill-mannered enough to mock a man in his eighties.

The main item on the agenda was about the sixteen gold coins in the museum. Known as the Golfodd Hoard, the coins were very rare, having been struck around the year 287 by a man called Carausius, who broke away from the Roman Empire and declared himself Emperor of Britain. He didn't last long, but when the legions came to get him somebody buried the coins, hoping to retrieve them later. He never came back, and the hoard lay in the earth for nearly two thousand years. In 1935 it was found by builders digging footings for a Golfodd housing scheme. Their boss, a local man, presented the coins to the town's museum. They were worth a fortune, being practically the only coins of Carausius ever found.

'We should send them away,' said one councillor. 'If the building's bombed, they'll either melt or be buried under tons of rubble, and if the Nazis invade they'll pinch them.'

A second councillor disagreed. 'Who'd bother to bomb Golfodd?' he asked. 'It isn't a port, there are no munitions factories, no railway yards, no coal mines. The Nazis aren't going to waste their bombs on us.'

'That's right,' agreed the mayor, 'and as for invasion, I consider it downright unpatriotic even to imagine such a thing succeeding. I say we keep the hoard here.' He drew himself up. 'It's our gold: *Golfodd's* gold, the most precious thing we've got. We will *never* let it go.'

The first speaker rose again, saying the coins ought to be sold to the British Museum. 'They've been after the darn things ever since they were dug up,' he said. 'Let *them* take the responsibility.' But the hoard was Golfodd's pride and joy, and he was shouted down.

In the end a compromise was reached. The coins would remain in Golfodd, but not on display. They would be removed to the library stacks in the basement. There was a fireproof steel cabinet down there, with a lock. This course of action was easy to arrange and would cost nothing. What council could ask for more?

He'd made no contribution to the discussion, but by the time he walked up his garden path, the man who wasn't God was convinced it had all been his idea.

SIX

Think of Land Girls

While the town council debated the fate of the Golfodd Hoard, Gary Mossman sat at home in the middle of a family discussion. Gary's family was Mam, Grandad and eighteen-year-old brother Dylan. No Dad. His dad used to be stationmaster at the town's tiny railway station, Golfodd Spur. He'd been the porter as well, and the cleaner, and the ticket clerk. One day a pretty young woman got off the train with a return ticket. That afternoon the stationmaster sold himself a one-way ticket and the pair left on the four-fifteen, holding hands.

The discussion was about Dylan, who'd worked up at Ling Hill Farm since he was fourteen. Now that war had come he was keen to join up, but Mam and Grandad weren't happy.

'Farming's a vital job, love,' said Mam. 'People got to eat, see, even in wartime. If you stay put, you'll probably not be called.'

Grandad nodded. 'That's right, son. Farmers were exempt in the last war.' He rubbed his left leg, the one with the shell fragments in it. 'If I'd gone farming, I wouldn't be a ruddy cripple, would I? And besides . . .' He winked at his grandson. 'Think of land girls, Dylan. They'll send land girls like they did in 1914, to help on the farms. The countryside'll ooze with floozies, all homesick and looking for comfort, and there you'll be with your big brown arms and a broad shoulder to cry on. They'll be queueing up.'

'Dad!' Fan Mossman frowned at her father–in-law. 'What a thing to say to your grandson. And what a way to talk about land girls. Floozies, indeed! They were perfectly nice girls, most of them, doing their bit in the war.'

'Yes, and that's the point, isn't it?' argued Dylan. 'Fit young chap I'd be, doing work a girl could do while other lads're away fighting. No.' He shook his head. 'Soon as Mr Elt can find a replacement, I'm off.'

'And I'll be off too,' put in Gary, 'the day I'm old enough.'

Fan shook her head. 'I hope and pray it'll be over long before you're eighteen, love.' She sighed. 'Watch your grandad struggling over a stile if you think war's glorious. He's fifty-seven, looks seventy. War takes fine men and makes wrecks of them.'

'*Some* of them, Mam,' conceded Dylan. 'The unlucky ones. But we got to answer the call regardless – got to defend freedom and that, or where would we all be?'

His mother looked him in the eye. 'Listen, son: they told your grandad and his mates in 1914 they were fighting the war to end wars, yet here we are just twenty-five years later, at it again *and* against the same enemy. They tell us lies, nothing but lies. Listen to your family, not them.' She snorted. 'There's never any politicians in the forward trenches – ask your grandad.'

Sam Mossman spat into the fire. 'There's never any politicians *anywhere* that doesn't have hot and cold running water and someone to wipe their bums for 'em. Stay on the farm, son. And you . . .' He looked at Gary. 'Work hard at school, win a scholarship, go to college. Don't end up like me, crippled and doing night work for a pittance. That's the reward I've got for defending my country, and I'm one of the lucky ones. Thousands are forced to beg, or starve. And we were all promised a land fit for heroes to live in.' He pulled himself out of the chair, grunting with the effort. 'Talking of night work,' he said, 'I suppose I'd better be on my way.'

SEVEN

Better Than the Trenches

The building shared by the Golfodd public library and the museum was on High Street North, opposite the town hall. As Sam Mossman limped towards it that Monday evening, a group of councillors came down the town hall steps and walked off in various directions. One man spotted Sam and crossed the street to intercept him.

'Evening, Sam.'

'Oh – evening, Mr Liffey. Late sitting, is it?'

Hubert Liffey was Mayor of Golfodd. He nodded. 'Emergency meeting, the war and so on.'

'Ah.'

'You were mentioned, Sam. Your job, I mean.'

Sam looked quizzical. 'My job? What about my job, Mr Liffey?'

'It was decided to keep you on.'

'Keep me *on* – I don't follow. Thinking of giving me the push, was you?'

The mayor shook his head. 'Not the *push*, Sam. It's just that we're moving the coins for the duration of the war, and a certain councillor suggested laying you off till it's over.'

'*Did* he now?' growled Sam. 'And what did this *certain councillor* suggest I do after I was laid off – join the Army?'

'Of course not, Sam. Everybody knows you did your bit in the last lot. Anyway, he was voted down, so there you are.'

'And the coins – where will *they* be going, Mr Liffey?'

'Into the basement, Sam, that's all. There's a steel cabinet down there that locks, and you'll be a keyholder. We think they'll be safe enough.'

Wishing the watchman a quiet night, the mayor went on his way. Sam let himself into the library, locked the outer door and stumped up the stairs to the museum. The curator's cubicle had a battered armchair, and a window through which a watchful eye could be kept on the Golfodd Hoard. There was a poky kitchen with a kettle and a gas ring. Sam filled the kettle and put it on to boil. Then he lowered himself into the chair with his bad leg stuck straight out. The job didn't pay much and his quarters were hardly luxurious, but it was a thousand times better than the trenches.

EIGHT

Here's to the Führer

The war was nearly two weeks old and the twins were at school when a woman arrived at Ty Coch, ordered a gin and orange and asked for a room. The request took Libby Swaine by surprise. Few women took rooms at the inn, which catered mostly for commercial travellers, who were always male.

'How long will you be staying?' she asked, rotating the register on the bartop for the guest to sign herself in.

'I'm not sure,' said the woman, sounding London. 'A few days, I expect. Is that all right?'

'Of course.' Libby turned the register and glanced at the page. Jean Harlowe. She smiled. 'Like the film star, eh, Miss Harlowe?'

'Same name,' said the woman, 'different bank balance.' She raised her glass. 'Well – here's to the Führer.' She raised her glass and drank.

Libby went down into the cellar where her husband was working. 'We've got a guest,' she told him. 'A lady.'

The landlord raised his eyebrows. 'A lady: there's unusual for you.'

Libby chuckled. 'More unusual than you know, Ken. She's called Jean Harlowe, and she drank a toast to Hitler.'

'To *Hitler*?'

'Yes. She lifted her gin and orange and said *here's to the Führer*. I didn't know where to put myself.'

'You should've asked her to leave, Lib.' He straightened up. 'D'you want me to chuck her out?'

'No.' His wife shook her head. 'She can't have meant it, cariad. Her idea of a joke, I expect.'

'Yes, well, as long as she doesn't repeat it in front of our customers. *They* won't appreciate the joke, I can tell you.'

Libby smiled. 'I'm sure she realizes that, Ken. She talks London, by the way: wonder what she's doing in Golfodd?'

When Mary and Tom got home at half past four, Jean Harlowe was perched on a bar stool with her legs crossed, smoking. Salesmen would check in later, she had the place to herself.

'Who's the glamorous blonde?' Tom asked.

His father shook his head. 'That's not glamour, boy,' he growled, 'that's make-up. She's London, pally with Hitler.'

'What?'

'She toasted the Führer in gin. Ask your mam.'

Tom looked at Libby, who nodded. 'It's true, Tom, but obviously she meant it as a joke.'

'Oh, I dunno.' Tom frowned. 'Old Gilpin was telling us in assembly what a fifth columnist is, Mam. It's someone who's not German, but who sympathizes with the Nazis. He says anybody might be a fifth columnist: the milkman, chap down the street, anybody. Keep your eyes skinned, he says, don't trust strangers.'

'*She's* a stranger,' put in Mary. 'Blondie out there. What d'they call her, anyway?'

'Jean Harlowe,' said Libby, 'like the film star.'

'Highly unlikely,' growled Ken. 'She's made it up, if you ask me.'

'Well, there you are!' cried Tom. 'A stranger with something fishy about her. *Two* things: toasting Hitler and a phoney name. I vote we watch her.'

'No.' His father shook his head. 'Miss Harlowe is a guest at Ty Coch, Tom. Of *course* she's a stranger – most hotel guests are, they're people passing through. She might have a perfectly good reason for using a false name, if it *is* false, which we don't know for sure. And as for that toast, d'you really think someone working under-cover for the enemy would be so daft as to propose a toast to him in front of somebody she doesn't know from Adam?'

'Eve,' murmured Mary.

The landlord shot her a sharp glance. '*What?*'

'Eve.' Mary smiled. 'She doesn't know Mam from *Eve* – she'd hardly mistake her for Adam, would she?'

Her father looked her in the eye. 'Too clever for their own good, some people, young woman. The point I'm trying to make is that the lady in the bar is a guest. A paying customer. She is not to be spied on, or made to feel unwelcome in any way. Ty Coch doesn't have so many guests we can afford to offend one, even one with a twisted sense of humour.' He looked at each twin in turn. 'Is that clear to you both?'

'Yes, Dad,' they chorused, but as soon as his eyes were off them they exchanged a look they'd used between themselves since they were toddlers. It meant, *Yes, Dad, but we'll do what we think's best anyway.*

NINE

Watching Moss Grow

A Tuesday morning, early October. First breath of autumn. Mist veiled the sun, and beads of dew sparkled on hedgerow webs. The four friends dawdled towards school, dangling gas masks in cardboard boxes. The masks weren't a novelty these days, more of a nuisance really.

A month, and nothing had happened. Certainly not in Golfodd. Perhaps not anywhere, since the papers had taken to calling it *the phoney war*.

No kids had arrived from the cities, because

the cities weren't being bombed. No storm troopers had dropped out of the sky on parachutes. The Local Defence Volunteers stood ready with their pitchforks and shotguns, but the enemy stayed away.

In short, the whole thing was turning out to be a huge let-down.

Sniffing desperately for a whiff of drama, Gary punched his friend on the arm. 'Anything new with your glamorous lady spy, Tom?'

Tom pulled a face. 'Nothing much. We searched her room, found a ration book with her name on. It isn't Jean Harlowe, but we knew that already really. She's called Violet Weston, but there's no radio transmitter. She isn't signalling to enemy planes – not that there *are* any enemy planes. She hasn't even toasted the Führer since that first time. All she does is sit in the bar and chat with the customers, including your grandad.'

'She talks to my grandad?'

'Oh yes. Anything in trousers, Mam says.'

'He hasn't mentioned it at home.'

Tom grinned. 'Well, p'raps they're planning to run away together.'

'Like my dad, you mean?'

'No, I *didn't* mean that Gary, I wasn't even thinking about your dad. You're too *touchy*, man.'

'*You*'d be touchy if your dad went off on the four-fifteen with a curvy blonde and never came back. What do they talk about anyway, her and my grandad?'

Tom shrugged. 'I dunno, I don't get close enough to earwig.'

'Has she said anything to your mam and dad about what she's doing in Golfodd?'

'Oh yes. Reckons she's been sent by some organization in London to look at the town, see if it's a suitable place for evacuees. Mary followed her last Saturday. She walked through the park and passed by the school, the swimming baths and the library. Then she sat on a bench and scribbled in a notebook. Dead boring, wasn't it, Sis?'

Mary nodded glumly. 'Like watching moss grow.' She perked up. 'Something's happening *here* though – look.'

The school gateway was just ahead. A lorry was parked outside. A man on the back was handing down bricks to another chap, who was stacking them in a wheelbarrow. Mr Price who taught P.T. was standing by the gate, ushering pupils into the yard. 'Come on, you lot,' he growled as the four approached, 'hurry along, this isn't a circus.'

In the yard, nearly half the tarmac had been broken up and removed, leaving a long rectangle of bare earth. Men with picks and shovels were digging a shallow trench round the rectangle's four sides, gawped at by a fleet of kids.

'It's our shelter!' cried Dil. 'Wonder when it'll be ready?'

Gary grunted. 'No rush, is there? Nothing to shelter from but rain.'

'Hey, mister,' called Tom to one of the diggers, 'will it have a machine gun?'

The man straightened up and looked him in the eye. 'I'll give *you* a machine gun if there's any more of your cheek, boy: it's a *shelter*, not a blinking battleship.' Some of the kids laughed. Tom was picking out one to hit when the bell rang.

TEN

A Few Loose Ends

Tuesday evening, seven o'clock. Sam Mossman was on his way to work. He'd set off a bit early so he could pop in to the pub. He didn't usually, but a woman was staying at Ty Coch who'd chatted to him a couple of times, and he felt flattered. *She must be at least fifteen years younger than me*, he told himself, *and not bad-looking. And anyway, we're only talking: nothing wrong with that, is there?* Sam's wife had died some years ago. People referred to him as Old Sam but he was only fifty-seven, for goodness sake. Not too old to enjoy a bit of female company.

'Evening, Sam,' greeted the landlord as Sam walked into the bar. 'Pint of the usual?'

'Evening, Ken, yes please.' Jean was on a bar stool. She turned and smiled, and when Sam sat down in his usual corner she joined him, carrying her glass.

'Hello, Sam,' she said. 'How was your day?'

'*My* day?' Sam shrugged. 'All days're the same to me, Jean. How about you – what've *you* been up to?'

The woman pulled a face. 'Same old routine, Sam. Inspecting the town and its surroundings, making notes. I've just about finished, as a matter of fact.'

Sam looked at her. 'Not leaving just yet, I hope?'

Jean shrugged. 'Soon, I'm afraid. A few days. Some loose ends to tie up, my final report to prepare, then it's back to The Smoke.' The Smoke was Jean's term for London.

'Ah.' Sam stared into his pint. The woman slid a hand across the table to cover one of his. 'I'm going to miss our chats, Sam. It gets lonely, town after town and nobody knowing you.'

Sam laid his other hand over hers and squeezed. 'Must do, I suppose. I wish . . .'

'There's something I've been wanting to ask,' interrupted Jean. 'A favour.'

'*Anything*, Jean,' husked Sam.

'It's not for myself, it's for work. I'd like to get a closer look at the library and museum: behind the scenes, sort of thing. It'd help when I come to write my report.'

Sam frowned. 'Behind the scenes, Jean? I'm not sure what you mean.'

'Oh, you know: what's there that's not on display. In the library stacks, the museum store-rooms, places like that. Museums never display all their stuff at the same time. It'd mean I could present a more rounded picture of Golfodd – its educational facilities and so forth.' She smiled. 'Good for my career.'

Sam let go Jean's hand, picked up his tankard and drank. He seemed to be thinking. He wiped his lips with the back of his hand and nodded. 'I don't see why not,' he said slowly. 'Not tonight though: there's a whist-drive at the library, lots of folk about. Would early next week be soon enough?'

The woman smiled. 'Of *course* it would, you old darling. Shall we say Monday?'

'All right.' He glanced at the clock on the gantry. 'Gotta dash, Jean, sorry.'

'That's all right, Sam: we've all got our work to do, haven't we?'

She watched him limp towards the door. 'Couldn't dash if the place was on fire,' she growled. 'Silly old fool.'

ELEVEN

Funny Thing to Ask

Sam's shift ended at half past seven in the morning, after he'd let the cleaners in. He got home around ten to eight, and Fan had his breakfast ready. Dylan was at Ling Hill Farm already, and Gary was upstairs, getting his stuff together for school.

'Morning, Fan.' Sam crossed to the sink to wash his hands and face.

'Morning, Dad,' said his daughter-in-law. 'Quiet night?'

'Aye, once those pesky whist-players had gone.' He sat down, reached for the milk jug.

41

Fan chuckled. 'If those old biddies are the worst thing you ever have to face as a night watchman, I'll be content.'

'Hmm.' Sam dug in to his cornflakes. 'I hope they *are*, love, but I'm a bit uneasy about something else, or rather some*one* else.'

'Oh yes?' Fan cracked an egg into a bowl, whisked it with a fork. She smiled. 'It's not the glamorous blonde you've been seeing at Ty Coch, by any chance?'

Sam glanced up sharply. 'How do you know about *that*, Fan?'

Fan laughed. 'Golfodd's a small town, Dad. Things get around.'

'Hmm – so it would seem. And yes, it *is* about her, but not in the way you probably think. Jean and I have talked a few times, nothing more. She's only here for a short while: there'd be no sense getting involved. The thing is, she's asked me a favour and I've agreed, but I'm not sure I ought to have.'

Fan poured the egg into a saucepan and stirred. 'What sort of favour, Dad?'

'She's asked to see the library and museum one evening, when nobody else will be there.

Behind the scenes is the way she put it. The stacks, storerooms and so on. It's for her work, apparently.'

'Ooo,' murmured Fan. 'Funny thing to ask, isn't it? Still . . .' She dumped scrambled egg on a round of toast and brought it to the table. 'I don't suppose there's any harm in it, just as long as nobody from the council finds out.'

Sam shook his head. 'It's not *that* that worries me, love. I don't *know her*, see? Not really. I mean, what if she's one of those whatsit – fifth columnists: a German spy?'

'Never!' Fan shook her head. 'Gary says Tom Swaine told him your Jean said *here's to the Führer* in front of his mam. D'you think a spy would deliberately give herself away like that, Dad?'

Sam shrugged. 'No, I don't suppose she would, love. It's all this spy talk that's going around. Makes everybody suspicious of everybody else, doesn't it?' He took a forkful of egg. 'Forget I mentioned it, there's a love.'

Gary, eavesdropping outside the kitchen door, saw his mother nod. *You might forget it,*

43

Mam, he thought, *'cause you don't know your Jean's not a Jean but a Violet. It's for sure me and the gang aren't going to forget.*

TWELVE

Oh Yes There Is

Twenty past eight. Gary met the others at the crossroads, bursting with his news. He looked at Tom. 'You know I asked about your glamorous lady spy yesterday?'

Tom nodded. 'I remember: there's *still* nothing new.'

Gary smiled. 'Oh yes there is.'

'Oh no there isn't!' cried Mary, doing the old pantomime thing.

'No, *listen*.' Gary grabbed Tom's sleeve, making him stop. Dil and Mary stopped too. 'I heard Grandad talking to Mam, see? And

Grandad said *Jean* asked him to let her into the museum at night, and he said he would.'

Tom shrugged. 'You're not thrilling me, Gary, if that's what you hoped. Why would a spy be interested in our boring museum, eh?'

'I dunno, Tom, but she *is*.'

'Maybe she loves museums but hates crowds,' offered Dil. 'Wants the place to herself.'

'Yes,' Mary giggled. 'Or maybe she wants your *grandad* to herself, Gary.'

'All right,' growled Gary. 'If you lot can't be serious, I'll have to investigate by myself, that's all.'

'Investigate *what?*' demanded Tom. 'A woman in a museum after hours? Better alert the LDV, eh, Gary? Call out the Army. Hitler's having his invasion in the meeting room at Golfodd public library, tickets one and threepence.'

'*Shut up*, Tom, will you?' snarled Gary. 'I thought you was looking to get a bit of excitement out of this war. I thought we *all* were. This woman's a stranger, isn't she, acting queer? She's Violet but she calls herself Jean. Toasts the Führer. Chats up my grandad in a bar, gets him to do her a favour. She's *exactly* the sort of person old Gilpin warned us about in assembly.'

Dil nodded. 'You're right, Gary, she *is*. Maybe we should tell somebody, even if it turns out to be nothing.'

Gary shook his head. 'It's not as easy as that, Dil. Tell somebody my grandad's agreed to let a stranger into the museum he's supposed to be guarding, and he'll get the sack. No. I was going to suggest we watch *Jean's* every move from now on, outside school hours, I mean. If she's a spy she'll have a contact, all spies do. She'll meet him sometimes, or drop messages for him to pick up. We need to see her do this. *Then* we can tell somebody: when we have evidence.' He looked at the others. 'What d'you say?'

Tom shrugged. 'We could give it a try, I suppose. Better than listening to Sandy MacPherson playing his flipping organ on the wireless all night long.'

Dil and Mary agreed to give it a try as well. The four would meet this evening after tea, by the pond on the green. They wouldn't discuss their plans near the pond though: there might be an enemy submarine in it.

THIRTEEN

Like Hitler's Moustache

Pupils on school dinners weren't supposed to leave the playground at lunch time, but Dil wanted to ask her mother something. Annie Tenby worked at the library. It was next to St David's church on High Street North, you could see it from the school gateway. She'd only to cross High Street South, then East Road, and walk up past the church. With the playground in chaos due to the shelter, nobody was going to notice.

Her mother was behind the counter, checking in a pile of returns. 'Hello, Dilys,' she said, surprised. 'Is something the matter, love?'

'No, Mam, not really. I just wanted to ask you something.'

'Oh, then you'd better come through.' Annie lifted the counter flap. 'We'll use the office.'

'This is going to sound daft, Mam,' Dil began when they'd settled. 'I can't tell you why I'm asking, and I can't even tell you *why* I can't tell you.'

Her mother smiled. 'Then you'd best just come out with it, love.'

'Yes.' Dil cleared her throat. 'Well, it's about evacuees.'

'Evacuees?'

'Yes. Suppose they were thinking of sending children here, to Golfodd.'

'Who's *they*, Dilys?'

'Oh, I dunno – the Government or somebody. D'you think they'd send someone to come and look at the town first, spend a week or two making notes about what's here? D'you think that's how they do it, Mam?'

Her mother shook her head. 'I don't really know, Dilys, but it doesn't seem likely. I mean, the Government ... surely there are books, maps, directories. And the council – they could

49

telephone the council. I think they could find out most things without actually *sending* somebody.' She frowned. 'Why do you ask, love?'

Dil shook her head. 'That's what I can't tell you, Mam, sorry. And there's another thing.'

'Go on.'

'Can you think of anything in this building the Germans might be interested in?'

Annie snorted, glanced about her, lowered her voice. 'To be perfectly honest, Dilys, I'd be pressed to think of anything in this building *anybody* might be interested in. It's a small town library, small town museum. Personally, I wouldn't travel from *Chester* to visit the place, let alone Berlin.' She smiled. 'Unless I was mad keen on Roman coins, I suppose.'

'Right, Mam, well thanks.' Dil stood up. 'Better get back before I'm missed.'

Her mother laid a hand on the girl's wrist. 'Dilys?'

'What?'

'I suspect you're hunting spies, you and Gary Mossman and the Swaine twins. It's hardly surprising, folk talk of nothing else. All I'd say to you is be careful, Dilys. It's easy to suspect people. You'll find odd behaviour if you look for it: everybody's different. But if you point the finger at somebody, you don't know where it'll end. Bullies flock to helpless victims, people have died. Just be careful, love.'

Dil walked back to school, deep in thought. The woman calling herself Jean Harlowe was doing *something* in Golfodd, and probably not what she claimed to be doing. But if she was spying, why the library?

There'd been a clue in her mother's words, but Dil had failed to pick it up. Sometimes, the thing we seek is like Hitler's moustache: right under our nose.

FOURTEEN
Nettles and Dandelions

'What did you have for tea then, Gary?' asked Tom when they gathered by the pond. Food was always a popular topic with the four friends. When they'd been a bit younger, they'd often played the game of wondering what the King was having for dinner today. Chicken always featured: a whole one to himself of course, followed by a list of their own favourites such as fruit jellies, trifles and chocolate cake. They imagined His Majesty scoffing enormous helpings of these items, and the royal menu never included cabbage, prunes or sago pudding.

'Eggs and chips,' answered Gary. 'What about you?'

Mary wrinkled her nose. 'Salad sandwiches,' she sneered. 'Heaauuugh!' She bent forward, pretending to puke in the pond.

'We had muffins,' volunteered Dil, 'with butter and strawberry jam. My dad says food'll be strictly rationed soon, and we'll all be eating nettles and dandelions.'

'Oh good,' said Gary gloomily. 'Something to look forward to, then.'

Tom thought it was time they attended to the matter that had brought them here. 'If we crouch under those windows,' he nodded towards Ty Coch, 'we'll be able to watch Violet alias Jean in the bar. She was on her favourite stool when Mary and I came out.'

'Oooh, crumbs!' gulped Dil. 'I'd forgotten what we're supposed to be doing.' They approached the inn, keeping low, hidden by shrubs from anyone passing on High Street South.

Violet was talking to a chap in a check suit. She must have cracked a really good joke, because he nearly fell off his stool laughing. 'Shame we can't hear,' growled Gary.

Tom grinned. 'Don't worry: she's bound to tell it to your grandad, and he'll tell you.'

'Speak of the devil,' hissed Mary. Sam Mossman had just walked in. He nodded to the woman, who smiled and said something. Kenneth Swaine pulled Sam a pint. Sam carried the brimming tankard to a corner table, the woman followed him. Check Suit drained his glass and left the bar.

Crouching soon grew painful, especially since nothing much was happening. Sam and Jean/Violet talked across the table. A few men drifted in, one or two others drifted out. 'If this is spying,' growled Dil after a while, 'you can keep it.' The others agreed, so they crabbed sideways till they were clear of the windows. It was a relief to straighten up.

'Well, *that* was a great big waste of time,' grumbled Tom. 'What we gonna do now?'

There were no bright ideas. It was getting dark. They started chucking pebbles into the pond. Presently they saw Gary's grandad crossing East Road on his way to work. 'No Jean/Violet,' muttered Gary, 'so no conducted tour tonight.'

They were following the old man with their eyes when Check Suit appeared, going the same way.

'Hello,' said Dil, 'where's *he* off to, I wonder?' There was nothing beyond the library except open country, and it was a bit late to be going for a walk.

Gary shook his head. 'I dunno, Dil, but we're not busy – let's follow him and find out.'

So they did, walking on the other side of High Street so it wouldn't be obvious to the man if he glanced back. Reaching a point opposite the library, they saw that the night watchman had gone in and closed the door. Check Suit had walked a few yards past the building and was leaning on a lamppost, smoking a cigarette and gazing up at the lighted window of the curator's cubicle.

FIFTEEN

The Wrong Tree

'Hoi!' The youngsters jumped at the yell. 'Who's that breaching blackout regulations?' PC Oswald came striding down High Street North, his eyes on the bright window. He noticed them, stopped and looked at Gary. 'Young Mossman,' he growled. 'It'll be your grandad up there, won't it? Doesn't he know about the blackout? And what're you kids doing here anyway?'

Gary nodded. 'He knows, Mr Oswald: he must've forgotten. We were watching that chap over th—' He broke off. Check Suit had vanished.

There was nobody under the lamppost. 'Th–there was a man,' he stammered, 'acting funny. We tailed him. *He* was looking up at the window as well.' He smiled brightly. 'D'you want me to ring the bell, Mr Oswald, tell Grandad to draw the curtain?'

The constable shook his head. 'That's *my* job, laddie: your grandad won't forget again if I tell him.' He sighed. 'What I want the four of you to do is go home. Stop tailing people. Forget about spies. Play with Meccano or bath your dollies or whatever it is you used to do before this lot started.' He shook his head again. 'I don't know: everybody's a ruddy spy catcher these days, except those who are spies themselves. Just go *home*.' He set off across the road.

The friends watched him mount the library steps. 'Keen, isn't he?' muttered Gary. 'Poor old Grandad.'

Mary pulled a face. 'That chap disappeared pretty smartly though, didn't he? Not fond of policemen, I reckon.'

'Spies *aren't*,' said Tom. He barked a short laugh. 'They needn't worry though, the spies: old

Oswald's too busy spotting lighted windows to bother with *them*. Come on.'

They dawdled back, noticing how very dark it was now the street lamps no longer came on. Not exactly brilliant, the light from gas lamps, but the difference was amazing.

They were crossing East Road when Dil murmured, 'I've just had a thought.'

'Wow!' mocked Tom. 'First time ever, was it?'

'Shut up, Tom.' The girl kicked a pebble into the gutter. 'It's something my mam said at lunch time. She said she wouldn't even travel from *Chester* to visit Golfodd museum, *unless she was mad keen on Roman coins.*'

They were heading for the pond. The others looked at Dil. 'All right, Dil, we give up,' said Gary. 'What point are you making?'

Dil gazed at the black water. 'The point I'm making is, we might have been barking up the wrong tree. Suppose Jean/Violet isn't a German spy at all, but a *thief*, after the Golfodd Hoard?'

SIXTEEN

Danger Or No Danger

'Where you been, love?' It was half past seven. Annie Tenby was ironing in the kitchen. Dil hung her blazer on the newel post and went through. 'Nowhere, Mam, just hanging about. Where's Dad?'

Her mother folded a pillowcase and ran the iron over it again. 'He had to go back to the shop, some paperwork to do with rationing.' She pulled a face. 'Seems customers'll have to register at the shops they'll draw rations from, and not go anywhere else.'

Dil laughed. 'There *isn't* anywhere else in

Golfodd, Mam. For groceries, I mean. It's the Maypole or nowhere.' The Maypole was the town's grocery store, Dilys's father was manager there.

Annie nodded. 'I know, cariad, it's daft, but the politicians love rules and regulations – makes 'em feel important.'

Dil laughed again. 'Sounds like somebody we know.'

Annie frowned. 'That'll do from you, young woman. Did you want your dad for a particular reason?'

Dil nodded. 'Yes, Mam. You know the coins in the museum?'

'Course I do, love – what about them?'

'We think someone might be planning to pinch 'em.'

'We?' Annie dropped a handkerchief onto the stack of ironed clothes. 'Who's *we*, Dilys?'

'Tom and Mary, Gary and me. We shadowed a man, a stranger. He followed Gary's grandad to the library.'

Her mother sighed. 'It's no crime to go to the library, Dilys. And you've no business to be shadowing people in the blackout, especially strange men. You know how we worry about you.'

Dil nodded. 'You never stop telling me, Mam. Anyway, I was going to tell Dad they should send the coins away to London or somewhere, instead of just shoving 'em in the basement.'

Annie snorted. 'It's no use trying to tell your dad *anything*, love, you know that. It was his decision to put the coins in the basement, and he's proud of it. I wouldn't mention the matter to him at all if I were you, especially since you're almost certainly mistaken about this mysterious stranger.' She ironed the last item, threw it on the pile and shook her head. 'This war's got everybody suspecting everyone else, when really we're just the people we've always been.' She smiled. 'Leave it, love, there's a good girl.'

Dil sighed. 'All right, Mam, but he *was* acting strange, the man in the check suit.' *And we won't leave it*, she thought but didn't say. *There's something fishy going on, and we'll do whatever has to be done, danger or no danger.*

SEVENTEEN

Like Flanagan and Allen

'What did your dad say?' asked Gary as Dil joined him and the twins by the pond. It was ten to nine Thursday morning. Youngsters were converging on Golfodd School from all directions, walking or biking in along West Road, East Road, High Street North and South.

Dil pulled a face. 'I didn't see him, he was out. I told my mam, but she said not to mention it to Dad, I'd be wasting my breath. What about your grandad?'

Gary shook his head. 'Told me I have a vivid imagination. Check Suit's a travelling salesman, he says, putting up at Ty Coch like they all do. He wasn't following anybody, he was just having a look at the town. My mam said the same, so did Dylan.'

'We didn't get anywhere either,' grumbled Mary. 'According to our dad there are no spies in Golfodd, and no thieves. Told us to stop snooping and get on with being kids.'

'So nobody's going to do anything,' growled Tom. 'We can't even go to the police, old Oswald thinks we're making stuff up. Anybody got a bright idea?'

'How about a teacher?' suggested Dil. 'We could mention Jean Harlowe-Violet Weston to Mr Price. And Check Suit too. Or one of us could knock on Mr Gilpin's door.'

'The head?' Gary snorted. 'Rather you than me, Dil.'

'So what *do* we do, Gary – wait till the coins're gone, then say *we told you so*? Fat lot of point there'd be in *that*.'

They trailed despondently across the street and into the yard. The shelter was almost done, a thick concrete roof was taking shape. The P.T. teacher was on guard as usual, protecting the

63

workmen. Dil screwed up her courage and approached him. 'Excuse me, sir.'

'Yes, what is it, Dilys Tenby?' He sounded narky.

Dil gulped. 'I . . . there's two strangers, sir, a man and a woman, acting queer.'

'*Where?*' Price glanced around the playground. '*I* don't see anyone. Are they on the street, near the gate?'

Dil shook her head. 'No, sir, they're not here now. I mean they never *were* here, they're at Ty Coch, the woman says *here's to the Führer* and the man was leaning on a lamppost in a check suit.'

The teacher laughed. 'Sounds like the music hall, Dilys – a double act, like Flanagan and Allen. Run along, there's a good girl – the bell's ringing.'

Red in the face with fury, she rejoined her friends. 'He *laughed* at me,' she grated. '*Music hall*, he says. What's the point of telling us to look out for types acting queer, then laughing at us when we report one?'

She cooled down a bit in assembly. The head was droning on about danger: how some sorts of danger had to be faced, especially in these perilous times, but how some dangers could be avoided and ought to be. Dil suspected he was leading up to one of his favourite lectures: the one about the old mine, and she was right. 'It has been brought to my attention,' he said, 'that in spite of repeated warnings by myself and the class teachers, pupils of this school are still to be seen playing near the entrance to the mine, and even going inside. This is extremely dangerous, the roof could collapse at any time; a footfall might cause it, or a shout. Thousands of tons of rock would fall in an instant, there'd be no time to run, anybody inside would be crushed to death.'

Gilpin bored on, but Dil had stopped listening. She'd just had the bright idea Tom Swaine had asked for by the pond.

EIGHTEEN

Town Crier

'Why don't we take the coins ourselves?' Morning break, the four friends in a corner of the yard. Three pairs of eyes gazed at Dil.

'What're you *talking* about, you twerp?' asked Gary rudely. Gary was often rude – Councillor Tenby reckoned it was because there was no father at home.

'Take them *ourselves*, Dil?' murmured Tom.

'You mean, *steal* them?' gasped Mary.

Dil shook her head. 'Not *steal*. More like, take them to a place of safety.'

'Such as *where*?' demanded Gary.

'The old mine,' said Dil.

'Oh, that sort of place of safety. The sort with a million tons of stone waiting to squash us flat.'

'We've been in loads of times,' protested Dil. 'It never bothered you before.'

'No, it didn't,' the boy admitted, 'but it isn't only that, Dil. How would we get into the steel cabinet, or even into the *building*? And what about my grandad? If the hoard was gone he'd get the sack. The council wouldn't know the coins had been taken to a place of safety. It's a wizard idea, but it'd need a lot of planning.'

'So, we've four brains between us,' said Dil. 'Let's plan.'

As the four broke their huddle, Jean/Violet left the inn and crossed East Road, heading for the phone box near the church. There was a telephone at the inn for the use of guests, but there always seemed to be somebody loitering near it and she needed privacy. The public phone box was in plain view of anybody standing near the school gate, and it was her bad luck that Gary and his friends chose that moment to drift gateward.

'Hey, look!' Tom pointed. 'It's the gin-swilling film star, friend of the Führer. I do believe she's about to make a phone call.'

'Why isn't she using *our* phone?' wondered Mary aloud. 'The one by the bar.'

''Cause it's a *secret* call, that's why,' hissed Gary. 'Go listen in, Tom, quick.'

Tom was halfway across the road before it occurred to him to ask, *why me?* and by then it was too late. As the door of the box swung shut behind their suspect, he scraped sideways into the space between the box and the churchyard wall.

He heard the clang as the coins dropped, but wasn't sure the woman's voice would reach him. He needn't have worried: Jean/Violet proved to be one of those people who don't really need the phone if the person they're calling is less than a hundred miles away. The moment she was connected, she seemed to forget about the need for secrecy and started bawling into the mouthpiece like a town crier. This is what Tom heard:

'Neptune, is that you? It's Violet. No, there's

nobody here, just me. Yes, I've got him wrapped round my little finger and it's on, seven thirty. Yes, Terry's here, he's cased the joint, there's a window below ground level belonging to a ladies' lavatory. I know, it's unbelievable, not even wired. So, the daft old geezer shows me the basement, I get a call of nature, leave the window open and Bob's your uncle. Of course I can keep him out of the way, trust me. Pick a fast car, I'll join you where Terry said and we'll be gone before the yokels here know what's hit 'em. Thanks, Neptune: I always try to oblige. 'Bye.'

The receiver banged down. Tom stopped breathing as the woman shoved the door open and stepped out. He waited till she'd crossed East Road and disappeared inside Ty Coch, then hurried back to school as the bell signalled the end of break.

NINETEEN
An Orange Donkey

First period after break was Divinity with Miss Owen. The class was doing the conversion of Saint Paul on the road to Damascus. The children were working in groups of four to make mosaic pictures of the dramatic scene, using gummed paper in various colours. Groups were encouraged to discuss the project among themselves, speaking quietly. Mary Swaine's group was discussing something else entirely.

'She was talking to somebody called Neptune,' murmured Tom. 'Said *I've got him wrapped round my little finger*. I think she meant your grandad, Gary. She called him a daft old geezer. She's going to open a window below ground level. The library's got windows like that, round the back. Sounds like they're doing it tonight – her and this Neptune chap, and a bloke she called Terry. I reckon Terry's the man we call Check Suit.'

'*Tonight?*' gasped Mary. 'What can we do? We got to tell someone straightaway.'

'Yes, but *who*?' hissed Tom. 'We've tried everybody, they don't believe us.'

'We'll have to do what I said,' put in Dil. 'Take the coins ourselves.'

'What, *today*?' Gary shook his head. 'How the heck can we take 'em today, Dil? I told you: it takes *planning*, a thing like that.'

'Then let's get planning, boyo, *now*. You heard Tom – it's tonight. We gotta plan *now*, take the coins straight after school, get 'em to the mine.'

'Oh yeah!' Gary snorted. 'Just like that.'

'I hope you're talking about Saul of Tarsus, Gary Mossman,' snapped Miss Owen. 'Sounds like a heated discussion to me.'

'It *is*, miss,' said Gary. 'Dilys Tenby wants to use orange for the donkey. Saint Paul didn't have an orange donkey, did he, miss?'

The teacher pursed her lips. 'The Bible

doesn't mention it,' she said, 'and anyway I suspect it'd be a horse, rather than a donkey. I'd favour the chocolate brown if it were *my* mosaic – that or the grey.'

'Thanks, miss.' He looked at Dil. '*See* – told you!'

Miss Owen's gaze moved on. 'Your grandad's key,' murmured Dil. 'To the steel cabinet. Wag off at lunch time, get it. Straight after school we go to the library. I distract my mam, you slip down to the stacks, open the cabinet, grab the coins, lock it again, crawl out the window. Mary and Tom'll keep a lookout, signal to me when you're out. We can get to the mine and back before five. You put the key back, your grandad'll never know it's been gone. Nobody'll know the coins've gone either, till the gangster's moll finds out tonight.' She smiled faintly. 'How's *that* for a plan, eh?'

The three friends looked at her. 'That's pretty good, Dil,' breathed Mary, 'especially for a spur of the moment thing.'

'Absolutely wizard,' nodded Tom.

'Hmmm.' Gary stared at the blank paper that was supposed to have the beginnings of a mosaic on it. 'Not bad, for someone who thinks donkeys're orange.'

TWENTY
What If?

Dil had talked a slick plan. It all sounded so easy, the other three wondered why it hadn't occurred to them. There's a difference between talking and doing though, and Gary had a hairy forty minutes at lunch time, and no lunch.

He got away from the playground, that was the easy bit. The shelter was finished, workmen were tidying up, and Mr Price was having a hard time keeping pupils from getting inside the new building through one or other of its two doorways. The head had announced a strict rule against playing inside the shelter, or climbing on its flat roof. The teacher was too busy enforcing this rule to notice Gary Mossman slipping away.

It was getting inside the house that was hairy. His mother was at her part-time job down Davis's bakery so that was all right, but his grandad might be anywhere. Gary used the privet hedge as cover to inspect the garden and the front-room window. The old man wasn't in the garden, and nothing moved behind the window. He daren't lurk too long in case a nosy neighbour was watching, so he eased open the gate and crept up the path.

Reaching the corner of the house, he heard sounds coming from round the back. Sharp clicks, some rustling. He froze, listening. It didn't sound like the window-cleaner or birds, it was more like . . .

Pruning. He let out the breath he'd been holding. Grandad was using the secateurs, cutting back roses or raspberry canes. Autumn jobs. Gary whispered a grateful prayer and twisted his key in the front-door lock.

He listened in the hallway, then went upstairs fast. If the old chap came indoors, he'd have to roll under the bed in his own room and stay there till he went out again. *Yes, but what if he's finished pruning?* murmured a voice in Gary's head. *What if he stays in the house till Mam comes home?*

Shut up, snarled Gary. On a mission like this, *what if* had to be kept in its place.

Grandad's room was next to the bathroom. There was no lock, and Gary knew where the old man kept just about everything. He slipped in and peeped out of the window. Sam Mossman was busy among the raspberry canes.

There was a curtained alcove with a row of pegs. Grandad's clothes hung from these pegs, together with his ties, belts and braces. The belt he wore to work had a chain cinched to it with a ring on the end holding four keys. The newest key, the shiniest, fitted the lock of the steel cabinet in the library basement. The boy sneaked another peep through the window, then prised open the ring with his thumbnail and slid the bright key off. Pocketing it, he went out onto the landing and listened down the stairs. To his horror he heard the back door open. The old man was in the kitchen.

There was nothing to do but get out quick. He scuttled down the stairs, glad just for once that his grandad was lame. He heard the cold tap spurt; the old chap was rinsing his hands at the sink. The shush of water masked the sound of the front door opening. Gary slipped out, closed it softly and hurried down the path, not breathing till he'd put the hedge between himself and the house he'd just burgled.

TWENTY-ONE
Godforsaken Dump

At three thirty that Thursday afternoon, Terence Bracegirdle left Ty Coch and strolled up High Street North towards the library. Registered at the inn as Gerald Holbrook, he'd just spent an hour in a corner of the bar, pretending to write up orders in a battered notebook. If you want people to think you're a travelling salesman, you've got to behave like one. Now, work over for the day, Terry was off to see what there was to see in Golfodd.

A sign in the library foyer had a hand pointing up a flight of stone stairs and the word MUSEUM.

There was a flight going down as well, but it was roped off and another sign said PRIVATE. Bracegirdle noted this and went up.

He knew about the Golfodd Hoard: it was why he and Violet Weston were in this godforsaken dump of a town, but he didn't go straight to it. There was nobody in the cubicle at the top of the stairs but you never knew: somebody might be watching from somewhere. He started at the beginning, moving slowly, looking at everything and reading the labels, like somebody passing the time in a town that wasn't home.

It was like every small-town museum. There were old farming and quarrying implements, bits of Roman pottery, a battered desk from a Victorian classroom with initials carved all over it. There were stems from clay pipes, a flint axe-head, a wooden truncheon and a set of ancient handcuffs. A shop dummy wore a mayor's ceremonial dress, complete with tricorn hat and clunky gilt chain. Terry Bracegirdle hadn't the slightest interest in any of this tat. He was here to examine the glass case that held the coins, so that when he came next Monday night to pinch them, he'd know its exact position and what sort of lock it had.

He shuffled round the exhibition till he reached it, and stared. There were no coins: just a colour snapshot of them and a card that read:

EXHIBIT REMOVED TO A PLACE OF
SAFETY FOR DURATION OF WAR.

An old couple had appeared. They were over by the dummy mayor. Terry made his way to the stairs and descended without hurrying. The librarian was at her desk. He approached her. 'Excuse me?'

Annie Tenby smiled. 'How may I help you?'

'I'm interested in Roman antiquities,' said Terry. 'I'm in town for a few days and hoped to have a look at the famous Golfodd Hoard, but I see it's been removed. I suppose you couldn't tell me where it's been taken to?'

The librarian nodded. 'It hasn't been taken anywhere, it's locked away in the basement here, in case of bombs.' She gave him a rueful smile. 'I'm sorry you've had a wasted journey, sir.'

'Oh, that's all right,' said Terry. 'It hasn't been wasted. I've seen everything else and who knows – I might be back this way after the war.'

Annie Tenby smiled again. 'Let's hope so. Goodbye, sir.'

He wasn't worried, it could have been a lot worse. If the coins had been taken elsewhere, the whole operation would have been scuppered. As it was, the lock he'd be picking would be in the basement instead of upstairs in the museum. It actually made things easier: Violet wouldn't have to work as hard distracting the night watchman, who'd now be two floors above the scene of the action.

As Terry walked away from the desk, two kids entered the foyer. They looked familiar, though he couldn't quite place them. Then he remembered: he'd seen them last night, across the road, talking to that copper. The lad had pointed to where Terry had been standing a split second before.

By the door he turned, without knowing why. The girl was at the desk, talking to the helpful lady. The boy was ducking under the rope at the top of the basement stairs in spite of the sign saying PRIVATE. The librarian couldn't see him because the girl was blocking her view. An alarm bell rang in Terry's head. Something was going on. He glanced through the glass panel of the door and saw a third kid loitering on the step, looking shifty.

It was dusk outside. He decided to hang about, see what the brats were up to.

TWENTY-TWO
Little Bleaters

Dil glanced towards the stairs. Gary had disappeared, so he must have gone down. She turned back to her mother. 'So you don't fancy taking me to the Regal tonight, Mam?'

Annie Tenby shook her head. 'I told you, Dilys, your dad doesn't like surprises. If you'd mentioned it yesterday I could have warned him. He might even have come with us, he likes Will Hay. As it is he'd get upset, and it isn't worth it.'

'Can I go by myself then?'

'You know the answer to that, love. *You*,

walking home at ten o'clock in the blackout, alone? He'd have the LDV out.'

'Oh well.' She tried to sound disappointed. 'I just thought I'd ask.' She smiled. 'I'll see you at home then, Mam.'

Her mother nodded. 'Have the kettle on, there's a love.'

Dil turned to leave the desk. There was a notice board on the wall opposite the door. A man was standing there with his hands in his pockets, studying the notices. She couldn't see his face, but the suit was unmistakable. *What the heck's he doing here?* she wondered, her heart pounding. *They don't mean to rob the place at this time of day, surely?* She saw a brief scene in her head: Check Suit going downstairs, catching Gary squeezing through the window with the coins. She hurried towards the door to alert the twins.

Terry watched the girl leave. She looked frightened. All of this might have nothing to do with the business he and Violet were here to conduct, but he had a bad feeling about it. Could it be coincidence that three of the kids he'd spotted last night had decided to visit the library at this particular time? Terry didn't believe in coincidence. The girlie outside lived at Ty Coch, a fact which added to his unease. He waited till the two girls moved away from the door, then went through it himself.

He stood in shadow at one end of the top step. The girls were at the bottom, talking in whispers. As he watched, another kid appeared from the side of the building. Terry recognized the Ty Coch twin. *So*, he thought, *they're all here, the four of 'em. And one's in the basement where they've put the Golfodd Hoard. Curiouser and curiouser.* He didn't know what to do. *Wish Violet was here*, he thought. *Or better still, Neptune Lester.*

He was still dithering when the other lad showed up: the one who'd sneaked downstairs. He'd come from somewhere round the back. The others surrounded him, whispering and pointing. Terry realized the Ty Coch girl must have recognized him in the foyer. The lad glanced towards the library door and wrapped both arms round his satchel.

It was that defensive gesture which gave the game away. *The coins!* screamed a voice in Terry's skull. *The little bleaters've only gone and pinched the Golfodd Hoard.*

The youngsters were legging it, past the library and on up High Street North. Terence set off after them, bent on violence.

TWENTY-THREE
Claustrophobia

'He's after us!' gasped Tom.

'Maybe we should split up,' suggested Dil. 'Swop satchels so he won't know who's got the gold.'

'No need,' grunted Gary. 'He's old, we'll leave him for dead once we start up Ling Hill.'

They pelted up High Street North and took the track to Ling Hill Farm.

'He's still coming,' cried Mary.

'Not for much longer,' grunted Gary.

Terence Bracegirdle was struggling, but he daren't stop. Daren't let the youngsters out of his sight. He guessed they meant to hide the coins somewhere, and he didn't fancy telling Neptune Lester he'd no idea where. He and Violet must have made a mess of the operation already, or the blasted kids wouldn't have known the Golfodd Hoard was in danger. Neptune'd realize this the minute they contacted him, and he wouldn't be nice about it. Neptune Lester was never nice about anything, which was his parents' fault for landing him with that ridiculous name. *Neptune*, for heaven's sake. What sort of parents christen their kid Neptune? Mocked unmercifully at school he'd turned mean, battering any boy whose lips so much as twitched on hearing his name. The meanness had become ingrained, turning the embarrassed boy into a vicious, violent man, so that now the mention of his name inspired not mirth, but fear.

Terry was in pain, but he pictured Neptune's face if he had to admit he'd been outwitted by a bunch of kids, so he slogged on through the fading light.

Used to these hills, the youngsters took the slope in their stride. By the time they ran past Ling Hill Farm, Check Suit had fallen well behind. He still had them in his sight though, and Gary had to admit he'd underestimated the chap's stamina.

The mouth of the mine lay just before the top of the hill. The four friends made for it at top speed. 'He won't know we've gone in,' gasped Tom.

'He'll guess,' said Gary. 'The sign might scare him off but it might not. We need to get well in so he doesn't follow our light. I doubt if he's got a torch himself.'

Terry had no torch, and he didn't know there was a mine. Staggering towards the hilltop he expected to spot the kids on the downslope, but instead he came to a weathered board with a crudely painted skull and crossbones and the word DANGER. Just beyond the notice was a cave-like hole in the hillside. He groaned, knowing the youngsters must be underground.

Terry didn't like underground. Not even the London Underground, which he never used. Terry suffered from claustrophobia, a fear of enclosed spaces. For a minute his fear of Neptune Lester was stronger, so that he crept into the mouth of the mine feeling sick and sweaty. Far down the tunnel's throat he could see a feeble, shifting light. *They brought a torch*, he thought. *They always meant to hide the gold down here.*

Ten paces in he froze, one hand on a rotting prop. It was useless, he could go no further. Fear of the cave had swamped his fear of Neptune Lester. The torch's flicker had moved on: in front of him was nothing but suffocating blackness. Moaning, he turned and stumbled up the damp slope, gasping for what was left of the light.

He was almost out when it came roaring after him, shaking the floor. He cried out, half choked by the dusty thickness of its breath. In his mind it was a living thing: a dragon from the dungeon, come to drag him down. He emerged gibbering onto the hillside as the roof caved in behind him.

TWENTY-FOUR
A Few Stones

'*W*hat's *that?*' Mary grabbed her brother's arm. '*Listen!*'

They all heard the rumbling, there was no need to listen.

'Rockfall,' gasped Tom. 'The flipping roof's caved in.'

'No!' Mary went rigid, clamped onto him. 'Oh my God, *no*. I can't be trapped down here, I'd never *stand* it.'

'Put a sock in it, for Pete's sake,' snarled Gary. 'It's probably just one prop gone, a few stones. Used to happen all the time, doesn't mean we're trapped.'

Dil coughed. 'Air's full of dust though – must be a pretty big fall.'

Gary shone his torch back the way they'd come. 'Dust's nothing,' he snapped. 'Who cares about a bit of dust? Come on.'

He started back, following the pool of light from his torch. The others came in single file behind him, Mary first, whining into her hanky.

'Long way,' muttered Gary after a minute. 'Fall must be near the mouth.'

Seconds later it reared in front of them. Gary directed the torch beam upwards, searching for a gap at the top. There was no gap, the wall of slabs and rubble merged with the roof across the whole width of the road. The beam swung left, then right, finding no gap at either side. The collapse had sealed the mine completely.

'It can't be all that thick,' Gary forced himself to say. 'We're practically back at the mouth. Dig ourselves out in no time.'

Tom and Dil started at once, scrabbling at the shifting wall with their hands. Mary pulled the reserve torch out of her satchel and shone it where they were working. She saw how every time a stone was pulled out, the mass settled to fill the place. She began to wail.

'Better douse that torch, Mary,' snapped Gary, propping his own on a stone so it shone on the fall. 'This one won't last for ever.' At this the girl's wailing grew louder, but she switched off the torch and stuffed it back in her satchel. 'You could help, it'll give you something to think about.' He started pulling stones out of the fall, leaving a space for Mary to work at his side.

'I've *too much* to think about,' she yelled. 'I'm thinking I wish I'd never heard of the Golfodd flipping Hoard. I wish it'd stayed in the ground, then *we* wouldn't have to. We should've let Check Suit and his blonde floozie have it, 'cause what's it matter to *us* anyway? *Maaam!*' She slumped to the floor and buried her head in her hands.

The others didn't persevere for long. It was hopeless. Every slab they shifted was replaced at once. Their hands were skinned, their nails torn and bleeding. They stepped back, panting and coughing.

'That chap, Check Suit,' rasped Dil. 'He was close, he must've seen what happened. If we shout, maybe he'll hear us, know we're all right.'

Gary nodded. 'Worth a try. Come on.' They took it in turns, shouting *Helloooo!* as loudly as they could. Tom picked up a stone and banged it on the fall between shouts. He'd seen trapped miners do this in a film, and the sound had carried to the far side of the fall.

It was then he remembered that the miners had never been rescued. They'd died slowly, in the dark. He went on banging, but now he sobbed as well.

TWENTY-FIVE
Serve 'em Right

Now that he'd thrown up, Terry felt a bit better. He was still shaking though, still sweating. He stood on the hillside, watching dust roll out of the mine.

He was a thief, not a hero. As a boy he'd dreamed of becoming a hero, as all boys do. His idols had been the flying aces of the Great War: Manfred von Richthofen, Mick Mannock, Albert Ball. These men, and others like them, had tunics full of medals and were worshipped by the public. As he grew older though, Terry noticed that most of them shared one other distinction: they were dead.

The grown-up Terence Bracegirdle didn't want to be dead.

Thieving had its dangers but it rarely killed. Instead of a tunic full of medals, you got a suitcase full of jewels and a wallet full of cash, all without working too hard. It sounded good, so instead of learning to fly, Terry had learned to climb walls and wriggle through windows.

Now, as it grew dark, he stared at the mouth of the mine and wondered what to do.

On the other side of that rockfall were four kids. They were trapped. Only he knew they were there. A hero might try to dig them out, or at least call to them to hang on while he fetched help. But Terry was no hero. He couldn't bring himself to approach that great smoking mouth, let alone start shifting stuff that might drop a ton of roof on his head. And if he went for help, people would ask questions. What's your name? Why are you in Golfodd? What were you doing near the old mine?

And don't forget Neptune, he warned himself. *How would Neptune take it if I said, I had to get help, kids were entombed. I know what he'd say. He'd say, all kids'd be entombed if I had my way.*

Turn round and kneel down, Terry old son, while I blow half your head away with this pistol.

He couldn't dig, and he daren't alert the town. The coins were lost. All that was left was to hurry back to the inn, tell Violet the heist was off, pack up and scarper by the first available train, with nothing but Neptune's wrath to look forward to.

Those kids had stuck their beaks into stuff that was none of their business, now they were stuffed. Serve 'em right.

TWENTY-SIX
A Poke of Sherbet

They yelled themselves hoarse, though they probably wouldn't have heard any response if there'd been one. Terror had overcome them, so that their yells were interspersed with shrieks and cries of Mam. Their assault on the rockfall was without method: it had become a gasping, panic-driven scrabbling which achieved nothing except torn nails and bloody knuckles.

Gary was the first to get a measure of control over himself. Standing away from the fall, he inhaled deeply several times to curb his futile sobbing. *This is doing no good*, he told himself. *We could dig for ever and get nowhere.* He called out, pitting his wavery voice against the shrieks of his friends, and against the echoes that filled the chamber.

'Hey!' But it was lost in the din. He breathed in and tried again. 'Hey, *listen!*'

They stopped screaming, thinking he'd heard a response. 'We're shagging ourselves out,' he cried. 'Wasting batteries, using up the *air,* for all we know. Miners wait *quietly* to be rescued, so do submarine crews.'

'Did someone yell back?' croaked Mary. 'I thought you'd heard something.'

'No.' Gary shook his head. 'Only you lot. We gotta do better than this or we shan't *deserve* to survive, see?'

'*I* thought you'd heard something as well,' sniffled Dil. 'You better tell us what to do – it's your mine.'

Gary smiled briefly in spite of the situation. 'It's not *my* mine, just 'cause my great-grandad dug it. What we gotta do is keep a grip on ourselves, save our strength, save the batteries. If we sit down, we won't need light all the time, and we won't be taking great gulps of air. We might even have a finger or two left to count on when it's sums at school.'

Nobody laughed, but nobody was shrieking either.

The chamber was wide enough here for them to sit in a horseshoe, knees touching. 'Ready?' murmured Gary. He doused both torches. None of them had experienced total darkness before. It had a texture, like thick velvet. They were touching, yet they were totally invisible to one another. Mary wondered how long the torches would last, used one at a time, sparingly. The thought of being left without even the possibility of light made her moan out loud.

'Grub,' murmured Gary to distract her. 'We might need some grub if it takes 'em a while to break through. What have we got?'

There was some blind wriggling as pockets and satchels were groped. 'I got some juicy fruit chewing gum,' volunteered Dil. 'Five pieces, I think.'

'I have two ounces of aniseed balls,' said Tom.

'And I've got half a bar of Fry's chocolate,' offered Mary. 'It's raspberry cream.'

'Hmmm,' muttered Gary. 'All *I*'ve got is a poke of lemon sherbet and a stick of black spanish. Not exactly a banquet, is it? Shall I take charge of the stuff, ration it out if we're here for a bit: or would somebody else like to do it?'

Nobody else wanted the job. The meagre supplies were passed from hand to hand round the horseshoe till Gary had them all. He wrapped them in what he hoped was a fairly clean hanky, and put them in his satchel with the gold. A thought came to him and he chuckled.

'What's *funny*, for Pete's sake?' husked Tom.

'Oh, I was just thinking: we have a handful of cheap sweets and gold worth thousands of pounds, but now the sweets are precious and the gold's flipping useless.'

'Very funny,' snarled Tom. 'You're wasted here, boyo: you should be on the stage.'

'Yes, and I doesn't half wish I *was*,' sighed Gary.

TWENTY-SEVEN
Exit Stage Left

It was coming up to six o'clock when Terence Bracegirdle walked into the inn. He pinged the bell on the reception desk. Libby Swaine appeared, looking flustered.

'Yes, sir?'

'Prepare my bill, would you – I'm checking out. Oh, and could you look up the time of the next train from Golfodd Spur, please? I'll pop up and pack.'

'Certainly, sir. Sir?'

'What is it, Mrs Swaine?'

'You didn't happen to see my children as you came along, I suppose: the twins?'

Terry shook his head. ''Fraid not, love. Late home from school, are they?'

'*Very.*' The landlady hurried into her cubicle to do as he'd asked. Terry strolled along to the bar. To his relief, Violet Weston had the place to herself. She frowned at him.

'What on *earth* have you been doing, Terry? I was beginning to think you'd had your collar felt.'

Terry glanced around to make sure the land-lord wasn't about. 'Worse than that, Vi,' he murmured. 'We've got to scarper, *now.*'

'What're you *talking* about, you numbskull?' She stared at him. 'Don't tell me you've gone and let some bumpkin spot that you're more interested in the coins than a travelling salesman *ought* to be.'

He shook his head. 'The coins weren't *there*, Vi, and they're certainly not there now. If you don't fancy a five-year stretch in Holloway, go pack and settle your bill. I'll explain as we go.'

He hurried off upstairs. Violet sipped her drink, thinking. *Seem a bit funny, won't it – two of us leaving in a hurry when we're not supposed to know each other? So – skip the bill, chuck a few bits in a bag and exit stage left. Won't be the first time.*

She slipped by while the landlady was checking Terry out. They met on the corner of East Road and High Street South and set off towards the station. Their train was due to leave in six minutes, and Golfodd would never see either of them again.

TWENTY-EIGHT
A Fifty-Fifty Chance

Ernst Pfeiffer had the same boyhood heroes as Terence Bracegirdle. Like Terry, he noticed as he grew up that sooner or later most of these heroes had been killed, earning for themselves the same last decoration: the wooden cross.

The difference was that the prospect of death didn't put young Ernst off. He was determined to fly. He'd have joined the Air Force, but in 1920s Germany there *was* no Air Force. His country had lost the Great War, and Germany's conquerors had banned pilot training and the building of military aeroplanes. The only way a German boy could learn to fly was by joining a gliding club.

Ernst started gliding lessons when he was fourteen. He proved to be a natural. At sixteen he was an expert glider pilot. When a new German Air Force was formed a few years later, he applied for pilot training and was accepted. He was a brilliant pupil, passing out top of his entry. Soon he was in action in Spain, flying with the Kondor Legion in that country's civil war.

At the start of the Second World War, Ernst was flying in a crack unit of high-speed, high altitude photo–reconnaissance pilots, flying unarmed planes over enemy territory to photograph key installations such as docks, railway marshalling yards and fighter airfields. It was precision work and highly dangerous, of vital importance to the bomber force that would soon commence the task of obliterating these installations.

On the day Terence Bracegirdle fled Golfodd with his glamorous accomplice, leaving four children to die, Lieutenant Ernst Pfeiffer took off from a base in northern France. His task was to fly across the breadth of England and Wales, photograph the dock areas of Cardiff, Swansea and Liverpool, and make it back to base with his precious film. Doing their best to stop him would be dozens of British fighter planes and hundreds of anti-aircraft guns. A betting man would have given him no more than a fifty-fifty chance.

The outward flight went smoothly. Ernst maintained high altitude and maximum speed. No fighters appeared, no guns opened up.

The docks at Swansea, bathed in October sunlight, posed for the Lieutenant's camera. The ones at Cardiff did the same. It was when Ernst turned his plane's nose towards Liverpool that things started to go wrong.

It was neither British fighters nor anti-aircraft guns, but his engine. The temperature gauge had suddenly gone off the scale. The engine started to cough, to miss, to cough again. Black smoke poured from under the cowling, leaving a trail across the sky that even a dumkopf couldn't fail to see. Ernst juggled the controls, hoping the malfunction might clear itself. It didn't. The engine continued to fire intermittently. He was losing height.

Desperate to get the vital pictures back to base, the lieutenant strove to nurse his stricken machine home, but it was too far. Hundreds of miles too far. With an engine in this condition, even *he* couldn't keep the aircraft flying. A couple more minutes and he'd be too low to use his parachute.

As Gary Mossman was wriggling out of the library window twenty miles away and three thousand feet below, Lieutenant Pfeiffer blew off his cockpit canopy and baled out.

TWENTY-NINE
Utter Swine

'What time is it?' whispered Dil. Tom had the only watch, and it hadn't a luminous dial. Gary switched on his torch. Its light was feeble, but after the total blackness they'd endured for what felt like a very long time, it dazzled.

Tom squinted at his watch. 'Twenty-five past six.' Gary switched off. Green blobs swam in front of everybody's eyes. 'Is that *all*?' murmured Dil. 'I feel as if we've been here all night.'

'Me too,' said Mary. 'Is anybody thirsty, 'cause *I* am.'

They were all thirsty.

'We've nothing to drink,' said Gary, 'but a chew of juicy fruit might help. Anybody want a bit?'

Everybody wanted a bit. 'We better just have half a piece each,' cautioned Gary. 'We might get thirsty again before they get us out.' He took two pieces out of the packet, bit one in halves and passed one half to Mary, invisible on his right. The other piece went to Tom, who shared with Dil.

The bits were tiny, but the sharp flavour brought saliva to parched mouths. The four chewed the gum, swallowed the saliva.

'They'd be digging by now if Check Suit had told 'em where we are,' said Mary.

Gary nodded, though nobody could see him. 'I know, I wasn't going to mention it.'

Mary pulled an invisible face. 'Sorry, but I'm right, aren't I? They'd have come straightaway.'

'Yes, they would.' Gary sighed. 'It's unbelievable that somebody could just go off, leave people buried alive. *I* couldn't.'

'Neither could *I*,' snorted Tom. 'Fellow must be an utter swine. At least he didn't get the gold.'

'And they'll come anyway,' said Dil. 'They'll have started wondering where we are about two hours ago, especially my dad. They'll be looking for us. There might even be a search party with police and dogs and everything.'

'It's how long it takes 'em to think of the mine,' said Mary. 'We're all forbidden to play here, and *they* don't know we had the coins to hide—' She broke off, then said, 'Did you lock the cabinet after you took them, Gary?'

'Yes, Mary. That was the plan, so nobody would know the hoard had gone. They'll know soon enough as it turns out, because I haven't been able to put my grandad's key back.' He chuckled. 'When he finds the key's missing he'll have to report it, and they'll rush to check the cabinet. They'll find it empty, link it with our disappearance and decide *we've* pinched the Golfodd Hoard and gone off with it.'

'Which is true,' said Mary. 'D'you think your grandad might think of this place, Gary, seeing it belonged to his family?'

'Hard to say. He might, I suppose. And *somebody* will anyway, sooner or later. Especially after that assembly this morning. All we've got to do is hang on.'

'What *I* hope,' muttered Tom, 'is that we're

operating on *our* luck, not the gold's. Last time it was buried, it waited nearly two thousand years to be found.'

'Thanks for sharing that with us, Tom,' quavered his twin.

THIRTY
Brought Up By Wolves

'Bit soon to start worrying, Mam,' said Dylan. 'Come and finish your tea.' He blew on his own to cool it. 'You know what he's like – he'll be so busy spying on somebody he thinks is an enemy agent, he'll have lost track of the time. If he's not back by seven, I'll go look for him. All right?'

'Dylan's right, Fan,' said Sam. 'Only yesterday Gary was telling me some tale about a chap at the Ty Coch following me to work. *Check Suit*, he called him. Reckoned the bloke was after the Golfodd Hoard.' The old man shook his head. 'I told him he'd a vivid imagination, which he has. He'll be shadowing some other innocent chap now, him and those three pals of his. Come and sit down.'

'Damned inconsiderate, I call it.' Ivor Tenby paced the lounge, looking at his watch every few seconds while his wife stood gazing out of the window. It was dark outside. 'Going off straight from school without bothering to let us know. It'll be that Mossman boy at the back of it, you mark my words. He's like one of those kids they find in India, brought up by wolves.'

Annie Tenby turned, clutching a damp hand-kerchief. 'Stalking about muttering won't bring Dilys home,' she snapped. 'Or blaming other people. Why don't you phone the police station, report her missing?' She sobbed harshly. 'And why in *God's* name didn't I keep her at the library till I'd finished? We'd have walked home together and none of this would be happening.'

'All right, all right,' growled the councillor. 'I'll telephone to PC Oswald if it'll stop you blubbing, Annie, but Dilys *isn't* missing, she's *late*: unforgivably late, and it'll be woe betide her when

I get my hands on her. Twelve's not too old for a damn good hiding, you know.'

He went out to the hallway. As she heard him lift the receiver, a thought occurred to Annie. *The Regal. Dilys wanted me to take her to the Regal to see that Will Hay picture. I wonder . . .* She hurried out to the hallway herself.

Kenneth Swaine was standing at the living-room window in the tenants' quarters of the Ty Coch. It was twenty-five to seven. East Road lay half-invisible between its unlit gas lamps. He was watching out for the twins. Libby came in, flustered. 'Miss Harlowe's gone,' she said. 'Taken all her stuff, hasn't paid her bill. I never saw her leave.'

Her husband shook his head without leaving the window. 'Doesn't matter, cariad,' he murmured. 'It's the children I'm worried about.'

His wife snorted. 'D'you think I'm *not*, Ken? Don't you think it's strange, two guests leaving practically together at no notice, and Tom and Mary disappearing at the same time?'

'They haven't *disappeared*,' said Kenneth irritably. 'They're revelling in a novel situation, that's all. The war: to them it's a welcome break from the dullness of life in Golfodd. It's a glorious adventure, and they're off enjoying it. They'll turn up in God's good time, you'll see.'

His wife pulled a face. 'I can't help suspecting some sort of connection between two guests flitting suddenly, and the twins going off. I can't explain, but I'd feel easier in my mind if we mentioned it to the police, see what *they* think.'

The landlord sighed and nodded. 'Yes, all right, cariad, I'll give them a ring.' He smiled. 'Just don't *worry*, eh?'

THIRTY-ONE
A Neutral Country

The parachute drifted down through the sky. The lieutenant in the harness was thankful for the twilight, which deepened as he descended. If he'd baled out in the daytime his 'chute would have been spotted, and he'd have landed in the middle of an armed reception committee.

Ernst Pfeiffer had no intention of spending the rest of the war in a prisoner-of-war camp. He was coming down in Wales. If he walked west he would eventually reach the Welsh coast and the Irish Sea. Ireland was a neutral country. If he could steal a boat and sail it to Ireland, he would be returned to Germany to go on flying. The hardest part would be crossing many miles of enemy territory without being seen.

He came down hard, slamming into the springy turf of a hillside. He lay for a minute or two, winded, straining his ears for any sound which might mean somebody was approaching. There was only the wind in the grass, and the rustle of his collapsed parachute.

Once free of the harness, the 'chute became his first problem. It was big, and it was white. Left on the hillside, it would be noticed at first light tomorrow, and its finder would know that a man had landed here and was at large. He must hide it.

He looked round for a good place, but could see no more than a few metres. There was a rocky outcrop a little way down the slope. It was the only feature, and it would have to do. Working quickly, he gathered in the silken folds and carried them downhill. At the base of the outcrop lay a scatter of loose stones. He knelt and threw some of these aside till he had a shallow depression. He crammed the screwed-up 'chute into this and piled the stones on top. He got up and walked round the little cairn, looking at it from various angles. It wasn't good, but at least when he'd repositioned a few stones no white could be seen.

The next question was, which way was west? As a pilot, the lieutenant knew how to navigate by the stars, but clouds blanketed the sky and denied him that option. There was a light wind though, and Ernst knew that Britain got most of its weather from the west. He turned his face into the wind and set off in his clumpy flying boots, hoping for the best.

THIRTY-TWO
The Willies

A wobbly voice came out of the dark. 'What time is it, Tom?'

Tom sighed. 'About five minutes after the last time you asked, Mary.'

'It *can't* be, that was ages ago.'

The boy sighed again. 'Light please, Gary.' The torch clicked on. 'It's twenty-five to eight,' said Tom. 'Count up to ten thousand before you ask again.'

'Nobody's coming, are they?' Mary began to weep softly, the sound of it loud in the blackness.

Tom found her shoulder with his hand and squeezed gently. ''*Course* they're coming, Sis. We got to give 'em time, that's all. They're searching, but there's loads of places we could be besides here.'

'Wish I was *in* one of 'em,' whined Dil.

'Oh, now don't *you* start,' snapped Gary. 'We could *all* break down and start screaming again, and it wouldn't do the slightest good. What we gotta do is keep calm, see? That way, we gives ourselves the best possible chance.'

'How's *that*, Gary?' queried Tom.

'Well, for one thing we can *listen*. Listen for people calling to us. We could easily miss a sound like that, screaming for our mams. And we can *think*. How to find water, for instance. A man can live a month or more without food, but he's a goner in four days without water.'

Tom grunted. 'You think we might be here four *days*, do you?'

'Maybe, you never know.'

'We *can't* be,' shrieked Mary. 'I'll go mad and die.'

'Oh, goody,' snarled Gary. 'Then the rest of us can *eat* you.'

At this the girl's shrieks grew louder, echoing round the cavern. Dil found her by touch and clamped her in a bear-hug. 'Ignore him, cariad,' she soothed, 'he's just a cruel pig.'

'Yes,' put in Tom, 'there was no need for that, Gary. You know she's never liked the mine.'

'I don't like it much myself,' retorted Gary, 'but we're here, and screaming'll give us *all* the willies.'

Rocked in Dil's arms, Mary quietened, till all that could be heard was a snuffle from a moist nose and the occasional stifled sob. They sat on bruised bottoms, waiting for sounds of rescue.

'Hello, is that PC Oswald?'

'Speaking. How can I help, sir?'

'It's Kenneth Swaine at Ty Coch. Look, I'm not sure this is a police matter, but my wife and I are extremely worried about our twins. It's eight o'clock and they haven't come home, and what with the blackout and everything . . . Yes, yes, I *do* realize the kids have taken to spy-spotting, and they may be following some innocent citizen right now, but there's something else. Two of our guests left unexpectedly this evening, and my

121

wife thinks ... Yes, two. Chap called Gerald
Holbrook, woman called Jean Harlowe, if that's
her right name. Woman left without settling her
bill. Train, I expect: Holbrook enquired about
trains. Yes, I'll hold the line.'

The landlord cupped a hand over the mouthpiece, turned to his wife. 'It sounds as though our
departed guests might be known to the police,
cariad,' he said. 'Oswald's gone to check with
Sergeant Thomas.'

THIRTY-THREE
The Trident Gang

Gary's brother Dylan was getting into his jacket when his grandfather said, 'Hang on a minute, boyo – I'm coming with you.' Tea was over long ago, and there was still no sign of Gary.

As Sam pulled himself out of his chair Fan said, 'What about work, Dad: don't make yourself late now.'

'Work?' The old man looked at his daughter-in-law. 'You don't think I'd go off to work and leave you to fret, do you, Fan? I'll get my coat.' He hobbled out of the kitchen. Fan started to clear the table, fighting back tears.

Dylan came and put his arm round her. 'It'll be all right, Mam, you'll see. We'll have him back in no time, Grandad and me.' He gave her a squeeze. 'You mustn't give 'im no tea though, Mam, worrying us all like this.'

Fan pulled a hanky out of her pinny pocket and blew her nose. 'I'd cook his favourite tea for him at midnight, love, if he was here to enjoy it.'

Sam appeared with his coat. He looked worried. 'Something up, Grandad?' asked Dylan.

'The new key's gone from my ring,' he croaked. 'The one that opens the steel cabinet with the hoard in it. I'm responsible. If someone uses that key to pinch the gold, I'm sunk. Got to alert the police right away. Come on, Dylan.'

Sergeant Thomas gazed at the two sets of parents besieging his front desk. He'd seldom known the place so busy.

Kenneth Swaine was at the front. 'You're saying that woman and Holbrook – *Weston and Bracegirdle*, I mean – are part of a London *gang*, Sergeant?'

Thomas nodded gravely. ''Fraid so, sir.

Headquarters recognized them immediately from your description. Known as *The Trident Gang* 'cause their boss is a villain called Neptune Lester.' He smiled briefly. '*Neptune – Trident*: d'you see, sir?'

'Yes, yes, of *course* I see, but what *we* all want to know is, are they *dangerous*, Sergeant?'

Thomas shrugged. 'They're thieves, sir. Jewel thieves. Professionals. They've never killed, as far as we know.'

'D'you think they've hurt our *children*?' demanded Councillor Tenby.

'Hard to say, sir, at this stage. I don't see why they would, and they certainly didn't kidnap four kids by herding them onto a train.' He frowned. 'Beats me what they were doing in Golfodd anyway, bunch of professional jewel thieves.' He shook his head. 'But I doubt there's any connection between them and the disappearance of your children.'

'My daughter told me she and her friends suspected them of being after the Golfodd Hoard,' said Annie Tenby.

Her husband rounded on her, spluttering, 'You didn't tell *me* anything about—'

'Yes,' cut in Libby Swaine. 'Our twins told us the same thing, Sergeant.'

The policeman nodded. 'Well, yes, I suppose the Golfodd Hoard *might* attract someone like the Trident Gang, but if so they've left without making any attempt to—'

'Excuse me?' Everybody turned towards the door. Sam Mossman had just barged in with Dylan. Thomas looked at the pair. 'What's up, Mr Mossman?'

'Two things is up,' growled Sam. 'Our Gary's missing, and so's my key to the steel cabinet down the library. That's the one with the gold.' He pulled a face. 'If it's still there, I mean.'

THIRTY-FOUR
Turn the Bike Round

G olfodd's two-man police force had no car, just
a bicycle. Sergeant Thomas turned to
Constable Oswald. 'Turn the bike round,' he
rapped. The constable hurried away, and the
sergeant looked at Annie Tenby. 'You keep the
library key, I suppose?'

'Y . . . yes, Sergeant, it's here somewhere.' She
fished about in her purse. 'Here it is.'

Thomas took it out to Constable Oswald,
poised astride his machine. 'Get down the library,
quick-sticks. Find the cabinet Sam Mossman
mentioned, check it hasn't been tampered with.'

He paused for a moment, thinking. 'You better drop by the mayor's house on your way, he's got the other key. Borrow it, but don't tell him why you need it. Off you go.' Oswald streaked away, ringing his bell. Sergeant Thomas returned to the desk to face the worried parents.

The mayor was not pleased at being disturbed. 'What d'you need *my* key for?' he demanded. 'There's a night watchman at the library with one exactly like it.'

PC Oswald decided not to tell Hubert Liffey there was no night watchman at the library this evening. 'Police business, sir,' he said gruffly. 'I'm not at liberty to discuss it.'

'Ha!' The mayor handed him the key. 'I'm the Mayor of Golfodd,' he growled. 'I think I've a right to be kept informed of events affecting the town.'

'My sergeant will keep you informed, sir,' said Oswald smoothly, 'as soon as there's anything to keep you informed *about*.' He pedalled away through the blackout, up High Street South and across the junction onto High Street North.

The library was in darkness. The steel cabinet

was locked, which was a great relief to the constable. He unlocked it and found it empty, which was not. He ran to the bike and set off back.

'It's *empty*, Sarge!' he cried as he burst into the station.

'*Empty?*' The sergeant's jaw dropped. 'You mean the Golfodd Hoard's *gone?*'

' 'Fraid so, Sarge. Whoever took it must've had a key, because I found the cabinet locked.'

'It's the Mossman boy,' grated Ivor Tenby. 'It *must* be, don't you see? He took his grandad's key and stole the hoard. He must have talked my Dilys into it, and the Swaine twins too.' He turned on Sam Mossman. 'You know Gary's taken the gold, and *that*'s why we can't find our children – they've run off with it.'

THIRTY-FIVE
Just Discreet, Isn't It?

In the hills a few miles from Golfodd, a farm worker was out after rabbits. He had a ferret in his pocket and a terrier at his heel. Suddenly the terrier, whose name was Mopsy and who ought to have known better, ran out ahead, yapping.

'Come 'ere, Mopsy, damn ye!' cursed the poacher. He'd recently done a month inside and wasn't ready for another. But Mopsy had picked up an interesting scent and paid no heed. Her master hurried forward, muttering to himself.

The aircraft lay crumpled in a hollow. It hadn't burned, but parts had become detached on impact. There was a wheel, a buckled aluminium panel, some tangled cables. Mopsy was interested in the wheel, but the poacher's eyes were drawn to a large black cross painted on the plane's bulged flank.

'A Gerry!' he hissed, glancing about him as if the pilot might come leaping out of the dark. 'Wonder if . . . ?'

Satisfied he was alone, the poacher clambered onto a wing and peered into the cockpit. It was unoccupied. There was a strong fuelly smell so he jumped down, moved off a few yards and stood gazing at the wreck, wondering what to do.

He ought to report his find, he knew that. Trouble was, they'd ask him stuff. *Where exactly is this plane? What time was it when you found it? And what were you doing out there at that time of night?* The last one was the hard one, of course.

Reaching a decision, he put Mopsy on the lead and walked a mile downhill to a phone box he knew of, just outside a village. There he dialled 999.

'Is that the police? I want to report a crashed Gerry aeroplane. D'you know Urch Hill? Well, the plane's in that little dip between Urch Hill and

Delf Hill, where all the rabbits are. Never mind who I am, I wish to remain anonymous. I'm not bein' cheeky, Sergeant, just discreet, isn't it? Good night.'

THIRTY-SIX
Stale Droppings

As Golfodd's tiny police force strove to cope with stolen gold, distraught parents and lost children, a squad of colleagues twenty miles away found themselves in the middle of nowhere, gawping at the wreck of a crashed enemy plane. The inspector in charge of the squad wasn't sure what he was supposed to do. He'd had a search made of the immediate area, but his men had failed to find any trace of the pilot. To the inspector, the crash didn't look survivable, but then he knew nothing about aeroplanes, and it seemed *somebody* had got out and walked away.

He decided to mobilize the nearest Local Defence Volunteer unit to start a search for the German airman, and the RAF to come and deal with the aircraft itself. The local rag was bound to print a story, and he didn't want crowds of sight-seers coming up here, pinching bits of plane as souvenirs and frightening the sheep. He slid a bit of torn wing into his pocket to impress his kids with, and the squad settled down to wait for the LDV.

Lieutenant Ernst Pfeiffer was discovering that fly-ing boots aren't designed for hiking. His heels had developed blisters, causing him to limp. The terrain was rough hill pasture – sheep country – and he was making far less progress than he'd hoped. He looked at the luminous dial of his watch. Was the time different here in England? The sun would follow its schedule no matter what they did to the clocks. He must look for a place to lie up before daylight caught him in the open.

He discovered what looked like a suitable place, and though dawn was still hours away, the state of his feet made him resolve to go no further tonight. He didn't know it, but the wind that blew through the tumbledown sheep shed was from the east, which meant he'd been limping painfully in the wrong direction.

The building had a damp earth floor and half a roof. A careful survey revealed no sign of recent human activity, though a pungent smell and a carpet of stale droppings showed that sheep still found the place useful.

The lieutenant cleared himself a corner under the roof and sat down, with his back to the wall and his pistol on the floor by his hand.

THIRTY-SEVEN
A Damn About Kids

A traveller going by train from Golfodd to London had to take a slow local and change at Shrewsbury. The war had made slow locals even slower, so that this first leg could take up to two and a half hours. Violet didn't mind. She was one of those people who can fall asleep anywhere, and so that's what she did. Terence would have liked to do the same, but every time he closed his eyes a short film started playing inside his head. The location was a hillside near Golfodd. The camera zoomed in on the mouth of a long-abandoned mine. As Terence watched, four kids ran into the mine. The camera moved closer, so that the viewer seemed about to go in after them. There came a roaring noise, and dust billowed out of the mine like smoke, rolling towards the camera, stopping the viewer in his tracks.

The scene changed. It was later. The camera was inside the mine, behind a massive rockfall. The four kids were screaming, tearing at the tumbled stones with bleeding hands. Exhausted, they slumped weeping to the floor where they'd die slowly from hunger, thirst and terror. Discarded nearby lay a satchel containing priceless, useless coins. The camera zoomed in on it as the screen faded to black. The film was a loop, so that every time it ended it started again.

As he watched the re-runs, Terence found himself crying. It wasn't that unusual – he *did* cry sometimes, when there was nobody to see him. On this busy train, he had to pretend to read a newspaper so he could hide behind it. What annoyed him was that he wasn't crying for the lost gold, but for the *kids*. Since when had Terence Bracegirdle given a damn about kids, for heaven's sake?

'I'm going soft in my old age,' he told himself.

'Neptune'd laugh himself sick if he could see me now.' He tried to pull himself together, but it was no use. The second he closed his eyes there were those kids again, dying slowly in the dark.

Which is why, as the pair waited at Shrewsbury for the London train, Terence gave his companion the slip and went in search of a phone box, where he dialled the number on a card he'd picked up at the inn.

THIRTY-EIGHT
Co-operation

It had taken all of Sergeant Thomas's experience with angry, frightened people to stop the three distraught families attacking one another right there in his police station.

'Anything could be happening to those kids while you stand yelling at each other,' he'd roared. That had shut them up. 'We need to get a search party organized,' he'd rapped. 'I'll telephone Captain Williams, get the LDV out, and I'll request assistance from other forces.' He'd looked at the parents. 'You'll want to help, of course, and you'll be welcome, provided you don't go back to fratching among yourselves: co-operation is what's needed in this sort of situation. You could start by thinking of places your children go that you know about – any dens, hideouts, gang headquarters – that sort of thing. Who else are they friends with? Can you talk to their parents and get them to ask their children if they know anything? And check whether any-thing's been taken from your homes: food, clothes, money. If they planned to be away for a time, they might have taken provisions.' He went into the cubicle where the phone was, leaving PC Oswald at the desk.

'Hello?' A group of boisterous soldiers surged past the phone box. Terry stuck a finger in his ear. 'Is that the Ty Coch?' Like many English visitors, he pronounced it *Tie Cock*.

'Yes, Kenneth Swaine speaking. Who's this?'

'Never mind. It's about those kids.'

'Our *twins*?' He cupped the mouthpiece and looked at his wife. 'Somebody about the twins!' he hissed. They'd dashed home to check whether anything was missing, and were about to return to the police station when the phone rang.

'Your twins and two others,' shouted Terry. 'Have they been found?'

'No, they bloody well haven't. Who are you?'

'Never mind who I am, listen. They're in a cave, just past a farm. The roof fell in. You got that?'

'Yes, I have, but how do you know . . . ? Hello?' There was a click as the caller hung up.

Nobody was sleeping. Stones make a poor bed, even if you're *not* half mad with terror. Gary's chirpy prophecy had proved false: they *hadn't* been found quickly. It was Friday morning, early, and the pre-dawn glow brought no relief down here. The blackness was suffocating, yet they daren't use a torch. They trembled, weakening.

What will we be, brooded Mary, *two thousand years from now? What will be left of us? Bones, that's what. Four little heaps of bones. No names, no feelings, no us. If somebody finds us, they won't know whose children we were, or how long we went on chucking ourselves at the wall, screaming. We'll be an interesting find, nothing more.*

'Mary, are you awake?' murmured her brother.

''Course. Who could sleep in this black hole?'

'What're you thinking about?'

She cackled drily. 'D'you really want to know?'

'I asked, didn't I?'

'OK. I'm thinking, if I lie flat on my back with my ankles crossed and my arms at my sides, and die, I'll stay in that *exact* position for ever.'

'Charming.'

'Well, you *did* ask.'

'If nobody's sleeping,' interrupted an invisible Gary, 'we might as well look for water. There's no night and day down yer anyway.'

'Where we gonna *look*?' groaned Dil, sitting up.

'Remember the time we decided to find the end of the mine?' asked Gary.

They all remembered.

'Well, we didn't quite, 'cause it suddenly got so low it'd be a squeeze for a badger, and the roof looked dodgy, and anyway it was nearly tea time. Remember?'

'We *said* we remember, boyo,' snarled Tom. 'Get on with it.'

'Well, that dodgy roof was dripping water. There was a muddy puddle on the floor. If we'd crawled in, we'd have got our knees filthy *and* been dripped on.'

'Not very intrepid, were we?' murmured Mary.

Gary shook his head, though nobody could see him. 'No, but at least we found water. Didn't matter at the time, of course, but it does now. I don't know about you lot, but *I'm* parched.'

They were all parched. The prospect of filling their mouths with cold water straight from the rock was irresistible, even in their demoralized condition. They hauled themselves to their feet. Gary switched on a torch. 'Come on, then.' They stumbled in a ragged line after the feeble light.

THIRTY-NINE
Close Enough

He'd slept, slumped in his corner. Now something had woken him. Sounds, not close but close enough. He grasped the pistol and got stiffly to his feet. It was broad daylight. Heavy cloud covered the sky he could see through the broken roof. He glanced at his watch. Nine fifteen. He was amazed he'd slept so long.

He flattened himself against a crumbling wall and looked out. The hillside before him was dotted with grazing sheep. Mist dimmed a tree-filled valley, and beyond it soared another hill. There were sheep on its flank, but there were people too: twenty or more in a ragged line that moved slowly downhill.

The lieutenant cursed softly. He was looking at a search party, and there could be little doubt as to who it was looking for. Either he'd been seen last night, or they'd found the parachute.

He thought quickly. *The hillsides are bare, I'd be spotted at once moving on them. I must go downhill and hope the mist hides me till I reach the valley. Among the trees I'll have a chance to dodge them.*

He moved immediately, crabbing diagonally across the slope and down. He forced himself to go slowly, so as not to frighten the sheep. If they ran, the movement would draw the searchers' eyes. He had his pistol, but it wouldn't help in this situation: they had more men than he had bullets, and some of them carried rifles.

He watched them as he moved downhill, listening for the shout that would mean he'd been spotted. They were calling to one another all the time in a casual way, which is what had woken him, but an alarm call would make a very different sound.

It was a fraught situation, because at the

moment hunter and hunted were actually moving *towards* each other. The lieutenant wondered briefly whether it might have been wiser to go uphill: once over the summit he'd have had the hill between himself and them, but he dismissed the thought. He'd have had to cross the skyline, and that's exactly what they'd be watching for.

As it was, his presence was still undetected when the searchers sank from sight behind the trees. It was the moment the lieutenant had been waiting for. He broke into a clumsy run, intent on reaching the wood before they did.

Under the trees he swerved right and slowed to a walk, following a shallow stream that chattered over pebbles along the valley bottom. He could hear the search party behind him, beating the bushes, calling to one another. He hoped they'd walk the width of the wood, not its length. If they saw the ruin he'd slept in, perhaps they'd climb the slope to investigate.

He stopped to listen. They didn't seem to be following him so he let himself walk more slowly. His heels felt raw. He knew that if he'd taken his boots off last night, he'd never have got them on again.

He was hungry and thirsty. He knelt beside the stream and scooped up water with his hand, sucking it out of his palm. At the same moment, a few miles away and deep inside a hill, four frightened children were drinking less copiously.

Hunger was less easily dealt with. After a mile or so, Ernst Pfeiffer found a tangle of brambles. Their fruiting season was almost at an end, but here and there among the wet leaves a few late berries glistened, drenched with dew. He stuck the pistol in his belt and plucked them thankfully, filling his mouth with sweet pulp till he'd picked them all. They weren't as good as a *grosse bockwurst mit kartoffel salat*, but they took the edge off his hunger.

He wiped his mouth with the back of a hand and looked up, straight into the eyes of an old woman with a basket on her arm.

FORTY

If Things Get Desperate

Another drip fell through the torch beam into Tom's cupped hand. 'That's your ten,' said Gary. 'Lick 'em up and make way for Dil.'

Tom licked the water out of his palm and stood up. Dil took his place, kneeling in the mud. She held out her hand. A few seconds passed, then a droplet fell. Gary kept the beam on the tooth of rock at whose tip the water slowly gathered. Four pairs of eyes watched the next drip forming.

'Blimey,' groaned Tom. 'It's like watching an icicle thaw. Why couldn't there be a proper little waterfall – we get enough rain, for goodness sake.'

148

Gary snorted. 'If this was a waterfall the mine'd *flood*, you twerp. Is that what you want?'

Tom shook his head. "Course not. All I meant was, if the stuff trickled down a bit faster we wouldn't have to wait so long for our turns.'

'I reckon we're lucky there's water here at *all*,' Gary replied. 'Think how thirsty you'd be by now if there wasn't.'

They'd been at the end of the mine for almost an hour, and had taken three turns each. Or they would have once Dil had caught her ten. 'Are we going round again?' asked Mary.

Gary shook his head. 'We need to be near the fall,' he said, 'for when they come to rescue us. They'll tap, and if nobody taps back they'll think we're under all that rock.'

'Shame we haven't got something to catch the drips in,' said Dil. 'We could leave it on the floor and it'd fill up, then we'd get a *real* drink.'

Gary nodded. 'I know, I've been thinking about that. I've got a pencil box in my satchel. It's wood, but I bet it'd hold water. I think I'll come back with it.'

'Worth a try,' said Mary. 'It'll hold a mouthful each at least.'

Dil's last drip fell. The four trudged back along the lumpy road, their knees plastered with mud. Gary fished out his pencil box. 'I'm off back. You three sit and listen. If you hear the slightest tap, start yelling your heads off. I *know* it could start another fall, but we'll just have to risk it. See you soon.'

They waited in the dark, saving the second torch. It seemed ages till they saw Gary's beam glancing off walls and roof. 'Listen,' he said as he rejoined them. 'I don't want you getting too excited, but when I was putting the pencil box in position, I thought I felt a slight draught coming from the mouth of the tunnel.'

'And you're afraid you might have caught a chill, is *that* it?' growled Tom.

'*No*, you moron, don't you *see*? A draught means air's getting into the tunnel. It means there must be some sort of passage to the *outside*. Trouble is, it's probably just a crack a mouse couldn't squeeze through.' He shrugged. 'Might be worth a dekko if things get desperate, though.'

FORTY-ONE

Why Not Wear Lederhosen?

The pilot and the old woman had startled each other. The lieutenant spoke first, in English. 'Good morning, madam.'

The mushroom gatherer stared at him. English wasn't *her* first language either. 'Good morning,' she replied, warily.

Ernst Pfeiffer smiled. 'I wonder if you can help me? My aeroplane was damaged and I had to bale out. I need to get back to RAF Valley. Will you be so kind as to direct me to the nearest road?'

'*Valley*, is it?' The woman shook her head. 'Long way from here, boy. You're on the mainland now.'

The pilot nodded. 'I know, madam, but once I'm on a road I can find a telephone and call my unit.'

'Valley, eh?' Pfeiffer's flying jacket gaped open, and the woman was peering at the insignia on the tunic thus revealed. This was an eagle, perched atop a disc that enclosed a swastika. The lieutenant cursed himself silently for his carelessness, and nodded as calmly as he could.

'Yes, RAF Valley.' He smiled. 'I'll be ready for a spot of breakfast by the time I get back, I can tell you.'

The woman nodded. 'I'm sure. Follow the stream. You'll come to a footbridge. Cross over, and follow the track down. It's a mile to the Golfodd road. Turn right. You'll find a telephone box a few hundred yards along.'

'Thank you, madam.' The lieutenant made a small bow, clicked his heels and wished at once that the earth might open up and swallow him. *First the gaping jacket, then the Teutonic gallantry. Why not wear lederhosen and slap your knees, you damned, damned fool.*

To his relief the old woman appeared to have

152

noticed nothing. She turned and shuffled away, seeking mushrooms.

Pfeiffer didn't want the Golfodd road, or any other road. As soon as the woman passed from sight he veered right, leaving the stream. It was hardly credible that the woman could have failed to notice his mistakes. So: he must alter course in case she put searchers on his tail.

When the Swaines burst into the police station, Sergeant Thomas was explaining to the Mossman and Tenby families why no police or LDV units were available to form a search party. There were reports of an enemy fugitive in the area, and everybody was out looking for him.

'It's all right,' panted Libby Swaine. 'There's been a phone call, we know where they are.'

'*Where?*' cried everybody at once.

'The old mine,' rapped Kenneth. 'He said a cave, but he meant the mine. The roof came down.'

'Who, sir?' asked the sergeant. 'Who made the call?'

'What the heck does it *matter*?' shrilled Libby. 'Our children are trapped underground, they've been there all night, we've got to get them out.'

'If the roof hasn't *crushed* them,' snarled Ivor Tenby. 'Should've been filled in long ago, that mine.' He stared venomously at Sam Mossman.

'We better get up there,' said the sergeant, heading off another row. He turned to Constable Oswald. 'You stay here, contact the mine rescue people at Oswestry. I doubt we'll get these kids out by ourselves. Come on.'

Dylan Mossman hadn't gone to work, so seven people followed Sergeant Thomas up High Street North. Sam and Dylan stopped off at the house to collect some tools, which they threw into a wheelbarrow. They worked quickly, aware that the children had been underground for far too long already.

FORTY-TWO

In Spite of Their Plight

'Are there any aniseed balls left?' asked Dil. She couldn't see Tom shaking his head, but she heard his soft 'Sorry, no.'

'We've eaten everything,' muttered Gary, as if they'd stuffed themselves at a banquet. 'There's just the water now.'

'I thought you said . . .'

'I *know*, Mary. I said they'd come and get us. I still believe that, only it's taking 'em longer than I expected.'

'How long can we last on little sips of water?' croaked Tom. 'That's what *I* wonder.'

'It's the batteries that matter,' reminded Dil. 'Without a torch, we probably wouldn't even be able to *find* the water.'

They were sitting so everybody touched somebody. In the stifling blackness, it was the only comfort.

Tom flashed a torch on his watch for half a second. 'They're just going into school,' he murmured. There was no time down here; it felt important to stay in touch with the world outside.

'Lucky beggars,' whispered Mary. 'I wouldn't care if it was double double maths, with extra maths at playtime, if only I was at school.'

'I wish I was waiting outside Gilpin's study for two on each hand,' said Gary, who'd suffered that legendary punishment more than once.

'I'd clean the floor in the boys' lavatories with my tongue,' murmured Dil. Somebody gagged.

'I could just fancy a school dinner,' said Tom.

'Ugh, *no*!' shuddered Gary. '*Now* you're being deliberately disgusting.'

They laughed in spite of their plight.

'Oh my God, *look* at it.' Annie Tenby halted at the mouth of the mine and pointed. The others

156

gazed. There were groans, whimpers. 'Those poor mites, stuck at the back of all that.'

'*If* we're lucky,' grated her husband. He scowled at Fan Mossman. 'Proud of yourself, are you?' Sam and Dylan weren't there yet, toiling uphill with the laden barrow.

'*Me?*' Fan scowled back, close to tears. 'Don't blame me, *Councillor*. My lad's in there too, you know, and I wasn't even *born* when this mine closed.' She drew breath. 'A decent council would have taken the place over long since, filled it in at the town's expense, but that's the killer word, isn't it: *expense*. Hold onto the money whatever happens. Well ...' She gestured towards the rockfall. '*This* is what happens, like in Hamelin.' She dashed forward with a sob, began clawing at the tumbled stones.

The others followed, tearing at the fall with their bare hands. Sam and Dylan arrived panting, grabbed tools from the barrow. Sergeant Thomas bellowed. 'Hang on a minute, everybody!' They looked at him. 'First thing is to communicate: let the children know we're yer. Pass me that pick, lad.' He took Dylan's pickaxe and struck a great slab seven times, the blows evenly spaced.

Everybody stood motionless, ears straining. There came no answering taps.

Fan Mossman burst into tears. The sergeant shook his head. 'Don't signify nothing, cariad: likely this slab don't go right through, sound didn't carry. Try again in a minute. Meantime, let's stay calm, tackle this in an organized way: don't want to make the situation worse before the rescue boys get yer, do we?'

FORTY-THREE
Jelly If We Have To

Terence Bracegirdle wasn't happy. It was a relief to have done the right thing by those Welsh nippers, of course, but he was dog-tired, and now he and Violet had been summoned to meet Neptune Lester at his favourite pub, The World Turned Upside Down, for what he called a de-briefing.

De-briefing, my foot, brooded Terry as he hurried past office buildings with sticky-taped windows and sandbagged doorways. *He's seething about those coins, he hates his operations being messed up, he'll probably have Vi and me knocked on the head and chucked in the river.*

Arriving right on time, he was surprised to be greeted by the boss with a pint and a smile. 'Why the long face, Terry?' chirped Neptune. 'Come and sit down.'

Violet was already there. She twinkled at Terry, obviously as relieved as he was. 'Neptune says it isn't as disastrous as we thought,' she told him. She turned to Lester. 'Tell him, boss.'

Neptune Lester took a pull from his schooner and dabbed froth off his lips with a big red hand-kerchief. 'Well, I'll admit I was livid when I got your call, Terry. *They've messed it up*, I said to myself, *after all my hard work. I'm gonna mess* them *up, so their own mothers won't recognize 'em.* I calmed down though, eventually, and I've been thinking.'

'What you been thinking, boss?' sucked up Terry. He felt light, as if he might float through the rest of the day like a toy balloon.

'Well, it sounds to me like those snooping kids had clocked you, Terry, and you, Vi. Oh – I don't blame *you*, I blame all this spy stuff everybody's rabbiting about. Anyway, they'd clocked you, and if we'd gone ahead and lifted the gold, they'd

160

have described you to the rozzers.' He smiled. 'Ring a few bells with the rozzers, your descriptions would, even out in sheep-country. They'd have told the Met, and we'd most likely have got our collars felt *and* lost the stuff.' He took another drink, employed the hanky and continued.

'As it is, those kids won't be giving descriptions to *anybody* now. A day or two and they'll kick the bucket, *if* they weren't squashed when the roof fell in. We know exactly where the gold is, and the war won't last for ever. When it's over we'll go back and dig it out, using jelly if we have to.' He sat back and beamed. 'How's *that* for smart, eh?'

'That's pretty *damn* smart, Neptune,' said Violet.

'Excuse me a minute,' mumbled Terry. He got up and staggered off towards the Gents.

'What's up with *him*?' asked Lester.

FORTY-FOUR

The Mention of Pants

'Time is it?' asked Gary listlessly.

A torch glimmered and Tom said, 'Ten past ten.'

'Sixteen and a half hours,' croaked Dil. 'Sixteen and a half flipping hours. They *know* we play in here, why hasn't somebody come to look?'

'Maybe they *have*,' murmured Mary. 'P'raps they said, *Oh, look, the roof's fallen so they can't be in there*, and went away again.'

'Thanks for that, Mary,' husked Gary. 'Whose turn is it to fetch the pencil box?'

'Mine,' mumbled Tom, 'but I don't feel very well. Can somebody else go?'

'I feel poorly as well,' said Dil.

'And me.' This from Mary.

'*None* of us feels well,' growled Gary. 'We're starving, for one thing. At least you lot had your school dinner yesterday, I missed mine getting that stupid key. It's twenty-seven hours since I ate anything, and *that* was only porridge.'

'I need to do number one *again*,' grumbled Dil. She got to her feet. Tom switched on the torch and handed it to her. There was a shallow alcove in the wall a few yards away. It was their lavatory. 'You should try to hang on,' said Gary. 'Our bodies need every drop of fluid they've got.'

'Yes, I *know* that,' grated Dil, 'but it won't do my body any good if it's in my pants, will it?'

Anywhere else, the mention of pants would have triggered a fit of the giggles, but nobody had the energy for giggling now. Dil shuffled off with the torch.

'Is she fetching the pencil box?' asked Mary.

'No, you twerp, she's gone to the lav,' snapped Gary. 'Don't you *listen*?'

But it wasn't a case of not listening. The four

didn't know it, but hunger, thirst and exhaustion were causing their systems to start to fail, little by little. They were becoming confused. A few minutes ago, Mary had thought herself in the Ty Coch cellars, where the beer was kept. At the same moment, her brother saw Reverend Pike approaching on a bicycle and actually called out to him. The minister melted away, and Tom disguised his call as a cough.

'Dil's a long time,' said Mary dreamily. 'I hope she's all right.'

'She is,' Gary told her. 'I saw her go further in, she probably thought she might as well fetch the pencil box.'

'Ah.' They fell silent, escaping into fantasies of sunlight, known voices, familiar faces.

They couldn't know that those voices, those faces, were no more than ten yards away on the other side of the fall.

FORTY-FIVE

Frightened Eyes

It was midday when the mine rescue team reached Golfodd. They found eight exhausted diggers and a pathetic mound of rubble they'd managed to shift with the barrow.

'Thank God you've come,' panted Sergeant Thomas. 'We move stuff away, and more slides down to take its place. The kids have been in there more than eighteen hours.'

The foreman nodded. 'It's knowing what to shift,' he said, 'and having the right tackle. Can you *hear* the children?'

Thomas shook his head. 'We keep tapping and

calling, but there's no answer.'

'Ah-ha.' The man made a quick examination of the fall, then turned to the families. 'Right, listen everybody. In a minute me and my men will start bringing equipment in here to shift this lot. It's heavy gear, and you don't need me to tell you speed's vital. I want you all to help by going outside now, and staying well away from the entrance. All right?'

'Are our children still . . . *well*, d'you think?' quavered Annie Tenby.

The foreman met her gaze. 'I can't possibly say at this stage, lady, I'm sorry. Eighteen hours isn't very long, but lack of water'll probably be a bit of a problem by now. That's why we need to start right away.'

Sergeant Thomas nodded. 'Yes, gotta give them room to work, isn't it? Come on.' The bedraggled group followed him out and loitered on the hillside, staring at the mouth of the mine.

Work started. Men moved to and fro. Encouraging sounds reached the anxious watchers on Ling Hill. Time passed. The weather was dry. The watchers sat down on the grass. The little stack of rubble they'd started grew higher, wider. They watched it grow, imagining the wall between the children and themselves becoming thinner.

One o'clock came, then two. *Twenty hours*, they thought. *Twenty hours without so much as a sip of water.*

At half past two, the foreman approached the watchers. 'The fall's wider than we'd hoped,' he told them. 'We're still not hearing the children. As I said before, water's a concern, plus we really need to let them know we're coming. So.' He gazed up the hillside. 'We're going to sink a shaft.'

Sam Mossman frowned. 'What sort of shaft – where?'

'A narrow one, sir, but wide enough to talk through and pass drinking water down, just till we get through the fall. We'll drill vertically from further up the hill. Our bit should break through the roof *beyond* the fall.'

Sam looked at the man. 'How d'you know it'll break through beyond the fall, and won't it bring the rest of the roof down?'

The man nodded. 'The answer to your first question is that we *can't* know: not for certain. We *hope* to break through beyond the fall.' He pulled a face. 'The answer to your second is there's a risk, but it's one we'll have to take, because those children need water *now*. I'll let you know the moment we break through to them.'

He strode away, feeling frightened eyes on his back. It was a feeling he was used to.

FORTY-SIX
No Choice, Cariad

The anxious watchers scrambled to their feet. Something was happening up by the drilling rig. Men milled about, gesticulating. The foreman had detached himself and was coming down towards them.

'They've found them!' cried Libby Swaine. '*Must* have.' She started up to meet him, but her husband saw the look on the foreman's face and caught her arm.

The man halted some yards short of them and beckoned to Sergeant Thomas. The two murmured together. Ivor Tenby strode towards them. 'What *is* it, Sergeant?' he demanded. 'If it's about our children, we've a right to know.'

The policeman looked past the councillor and spoke to the others. 'I'm sorry,' he told them. 'The foreman's news is bad. We both wish there was some way we could wrap it up so it sounded better, but there isn't. Fact is, the risk we had to take has turned out badly, and there's been a second roof-fall. We have to tell you that this greatly reduces the chance that the children will be found alive.'

Gary stepped back from the alcove and buttoned his fly. He was pulling the torch out of his pocket when he heard a grinding noise in the blackness above his head. He looked up and got a shower of grit in his face. Spitting and cursing, he switched on the torch and pointed it at the roof. The noise continued, and he saw fine debris sifting down through the beam. He turned to where the others were sitting.

'Get up you lot, *quick*!' he yelled. 'Roof's coming in.' He blinked the grit from his eyes as they came hobbling to his light. 'I can *feel* it,' cried Mary. 'It's landing in my hair.'

'Me too,' wobbled Tom. 'What can we *do*, Gary?'

'Only one thing left,' rasped Gary. 'The tunnel. We'll have to follow it, hope there's a decent-size crack at the far end. That draught's got to be coming from *somewhere*. Come on.'

He led the way. From behind came the patter of stones hitting the floor. 'It's *going*,' said Dil, bringing up the rear.

'Keep moving,' barked Gary.

The roof above them held. They reached the tunnel. Gary's pencil box lay on the mud in its mouth. He picked it up, drank from it and passed it to Mary. 'Might be the last drink for a bit,' he warned. They all drank. 'Right,' he said. 'I'll lead. Mary, you come second. I know you're scared: we're *all* scared, but this is for our *lives*, right? Dil follows Mary, and Tom's our tail-end Charlie. Let's go.'

He knelt in the mud and ducked into the opening. The tunnel was about two and a half feet high, lower where stones jutted from its glistening roof. He crawled forward, grazing his knees on the bumpy floor. The others followed.

'This is *horrible*,' sobbed Mary. 'I don't think I can go on, Gary.'

'You've no choice, cariad,' said Gary. 'The others can't get past you, and you can neither turn round nor squeeze past *them* crawling backwards. It'll be all right, you'll see.'

They moved slowly, banging their heads and faces on jutting stones. The tunnel was growing no wider, but it wasn't narrowing either. They knew that if it did, they'd die here.

FORTY-SEVEN
Ireland Next Stop

Broad daylight on a naked hillside, the mist lifting. From behind and below came sounds of pursuit. The old mushroom picker had noticed something after all, and the lieutenant needed a place to hide.

There were no trees up here. His pursuers were among the trees. He must move higher, risk breaking the skyline. On the far slope there'd be something, perhaps.

He scuttled in a crouch, like a goblin in one of Grimm's fairy tales, over the crest and down. This slope was bare as well, except for a low rocky feature down and to his left. It wasn't much of a feature; a few stones poked through the turf to form a rough circle round a shallow depression. It wasn't much, but it might have to do because the searchers were getting closer.

He squeezed into a cleft between two stones. Rushes grew in clumps across the depression, helping to conceal him. He watched the crest, hoping the soldiers would pass without noticing the stones.

They noticed, but evidently didn't believe the spot worth searching. One man – an elderly chap with Great War ribbons and a Great War rifle – came halfway towards the feature and stood for a moment, gazing at it. Ernst Pfeiffer curled his fingers round the grip of his pistol, hoping he wasn't going to have to shoot the old man. He sighed with relief when the chap turned and loped after his comrades.

Once the search party had passed, the lieutenant knew he'd be fairly safe unless a shepherd turned up. There were sheep all around, but with the lambing and shearing seasons long gone, it wasn't likely they'd be needing much attention. He made himself as comfortable as possible, and settled down to wait for darkness.

He slept, and when he woke it was dusk. He was cold, and ravenously hungry. He thought about his comrades, returned at this hour from their various missions. They'd peel off their flying suits, have showers and stroll across to the mess, where a warming meal would be served. They'd eat and yarn, boastfully about the day's actions, respectfully about comrades who had failed to return, including himself. He felt a pang, wishing he was with them.

I will be, he promised himself, *in a few days, by way of Ireland.* In the meantime though, he must have food. Earlier he'd passed a farm, skirting round it to avoid being seen. He'd go back under cover of darkness, see what he could find.

He was in luck: no dog barked at his approach. Nothing stirred in the yard. Because of the blackout, no light spilled from the house. Moonlight silvered the roof, that was all. It was a perfect night for thieving.

The doors of various outbuildings had no locks. Ernst Pfeiffer investigated them all, finding nothing a human might eat. There was a donkey, and he certainly felt hungry enough to eat that, but he stroked its ear instead and left it alone in case it decided to bray.

That left the house. The lieutenant circled it, seeking a way in. At one end was a lean-to porch with a door open to the yard. He peered in, saw a row of muddy boots and oilskin capes on hooks. When his eyes adjusted to the gloom he saw something better: two zinc buckets beside the inner door, one full of milk, the other full of eggs.

He drank as much milk as he dared, squatting by the bucket and scooping it up with his hand, watching the inner door every second: listening too. Full of milk, he filled all his pockets with eggs before helping himself to a yellow cape, a greasy flat cap and a pair of gumboots he thought might fit him.

Bulging with swag, he hurried back to his hiding place, to feast on raw eggs and bury his flying boots. The gumboots proved far more comfortable, the cape covered his uniform completely, and the cap made him look like a local.

He hadn't been able to pinch a mirror so he couldn't see himself, but he'd a fair idea what he looked like. He grinned in the dark. 'Ireland next stop,' he said.

FORTY-EIGHT
Crocodile

'You can't *stop*,' cried Libby Swaine. 'You'll go on trying, won't you? Our *children* . . .'

The foreman nodded. 'I *know*, lady, and I'd give anything to bring them out unhurt, but I can't lie to you. These nineteenth-century gold diggings were short: this one's suffered two falls, which probably means there's no roof left at all.' A tear trickled down his grimy cheek, leaving a pale track. 'No space where anybody could be *standing*, see?'

'An air pocket,' choked Annie Tenby. 'How d'you know there isn't an air pocket or – you

177

know – a branch off the main tunnel? God wouldn't let four innocent children die like this: you've heard of miracles in mines – men found alive in air pockets, long after they've been given up for dead.'

The man nodded. 'Yes, I have, and of *course* we'll go on trying. It's just . . . I don't want to raise false hope. If we reach them – and it's a big if – likely it'll be bodies we'll be fetching out. I'm sorry.'

Sam Mossman nodded. 'There's no branch,' he confirmed. 'It's one straight road, and a short one. And like the man says, it'll all have gone now.'

As the distraught families clung to one another, the foreman spoke to Sergeant Thomas. 'Get the poor devils to go home,' he murmured. 'Whatever we pull out of this mess won't be fit for them to see.'

The policeman spoke gently to the seven and led them downhill: a shuffling, broken crocodile, though the tears that fell were none of them crocodile tears.

As their families crept away, the four children moved far more slowly in the opposite direction.

Their knees were raw, their heads seeped blood from countless cuts and grazes, and they were so thirsty that they paused from time to time to lick the wet stone of the tunnel wall. Hunger gnawed their insides like starved rats, sapping their strength, but there was absolutely nothing they could do about that.

'What if this tunnel goes on for ever?' croaked Tom.

Gary scoffed. '*Nothing* goes on for ever, you twerp.'

'Except being dead,' muttered Dil.

'Thanks for that, Dil,' said Gary drily. 'I'm not worried about it going on for ever: we're bound to reach the end eventually. What worries me is if the end turns out to be a little crack or something: a gap too narrow for us to squeeze through.'

'If I get any hungrier,' moaned Mary, 'I'll be thin enough to squeeze through *any* crack.'

'Perhaps that's God's *plan*,' suggested Tom.

Gary chuckled. 'Complicated sort of plan, isn't it? I mean, why let the roof fall in the first place? He could've left it up and saved Himself all this trouble.'

Doggedly they dragged themselves forward over the cold, wet floor. Their talk of endless tunnels and narrow cracks was a way to avoid thinking about a more immediate worry. The torchlight was becoming weaker as the batteries started to fail. What if they flickered out altogether before the tunnel ended? Would their courage carry them onward in total blackness, or would they seize up and scream themselves to death?

FORTY-NINE
Bungling Cop

He walked through the night in his cap, cape and wellingtons, making fair progress. Nobody saw him, and if they had they'd have taken him for a poacher, or somebody wending home from a celebration.

Dawn found him on yet another hillside. This one was dotted with outcrops as well as sheep. There were stands of stunted scrub too: gorse and hawthorn. The lieutenant picked a spot where a hawthorn had writhed from between jutting stones, reaching for the sky. Here, he threw himself down on a springy, needlegrass bed. The rocks and autumn foliage would make him hard to spot, even for somebody passing close by.

For once, Ernst Pfeiffer was neither hungry nor cold. He was dead tired though, and soon fell asleep. He woke to a noise like machinery. It sounded dangerously close. He got up and crouched among foliage, listening.

It seemed to be coming from the far side of the hill. Muttering an oath, he left his hiding place and climbed to the top, crawling the last few feet.

Raising his head cautiously, he saw a knot of men halfway down the slope. They were standing round some sort of mechanical digger, and seemed to be starting a quarry. Mounds of earth and rubble lay about, and a flatbed truck was parked on the turf.

Too close, decided the lieutenant. *I must move, find a more private spot.* He sighed. *And I was hier sehr gemütlich.* He returned to the outcrop to gather his kit.

It was then he heard a sound that made his scalp crawl.

*   *   *

Richard Pritchard poked his head round the police station door. 'I wonder, have you got a minute, Sarge?'

'It's *Sergeant*,' growled Thomas, 'not Sarge. What d'you want, as if I didn't know.' Richard Pritchard was a reporter with the *Golfodd Gleaner*. In fact he was the paper's *only* reporter, and Sergeant Thomas didn't like him. The *Gleaner* was a weekly paper, came out every Thursday. By Friday night, most copies were to be found keeping packets of fish and chips warm. Richard Pritchard's ambition was to leave Golfodd behind for a job on one of the big papers in Manchester or London, and he believed the way to achieve this was to be as nosy and as nasty as possible.

'It's about the hoard,' he said. 'Are steps being taken to recover it?'

'The *hoard*?' Thomas stared at the reporter. 'You want to know about the coins, not the kids?'

Pritchard shrugged. 'I know about the kids: they're deceased. It'll be all over the nationals in the morning – no point putting it in next Thursday's *Gleaner*, is there? Missed the boat, see? Stale news.'

183

Thomas curled his lip. 'You're an animal, Pritchard. I've just taken those kids' mams and dads home, destroyed. And all you can think about is some rotten gold. Get out of my station before I *chuck* you out.'

The reporter raised his hands in a calming gesture. 'All right, boyo: if *you* won't talk to me, I'll go to *them*. Ask if *they* think the kids pinched the hoard, hid it in the mine.'

The sergeant was out from behind the desk in a flash. 'You go anywhere *near* those poor folk and I'll ring your scrawny neck for you, you bag of manure.'

The reporter backed to the door. 'What about the freedom of the press?' he whined.

'Freedom of my backside!' snarled the sergeant. 'If I catch you bothering those people, *or* the rescuers up at the mine, I'll make you wish your mother had drowned you at birth.'

Halfway out Pritchard paused, sketched an invisible headline in the air. 'GOLFODD'S LOST GOLD – BUNGLING COP THREATENS REPORTER.' He grinned. 'Next Thursday, Sarge: that's a promise.'

FIFTY
Calcium Carbonate

'Hey!' Gary had stopped crawling. 'I think we're at the end. Look, it opens up.' He moved the torch beam to show them. Mary scuttled forward, practically climbing on his back. 'I can see light!' she cried. 'Switch the torch off a sec.'

He switched off, and Mary was right. They weren't plunged into blackness. The vault that soared above them was suffused with a pearly grey light. It was weak, but it was the most wonderful light that had ever fallen on the cavers.

Tom called from the rear. 'Can you see the sky?'

Gary peered upwards, shook his head. 'No. It's a long way up by the look of it, and not straight. The light's reflecting off the wall. Hang on.' He moved forward and stood up, stiff as a pensioner. 'There's room for us all,' he said.

They stood in the thin glow, stretching cramped limbs. Mary whispered a prayer of thankfulness. Dil dabbed a bleeding knee with her hanky. Tom examined the wall, stroked its glistening surface with his hand. 'Smooth,' he muttered, 'like glass. Dunno how we'll climb out.'

Gary touched it with his fingertips. 'Hmmm. You know what it is, don't you?'

Tom shook his head. 'Not really, no.'

'Calcium carbonate – the stuff stalactites are made of.' He gazed up. 'There isn't bound to be a gap we can get through anyway.'

Dil snorted. 'It's being so cheerful that keeps you going, isn't it, Gary?'

'Why don't we shout?' suggested Mary. 'Someone might hear.'

Famished and exhausted as they were, they

tipped their heads back and sent the last of their energy echoing up the shaft.

The lieutenant froze, a gumboot dangling from his hand. *'Kinder?'* he whispered to himself. He could swear he'd heard children's voices, but there was nobody on the hillside. He shivered, imagining the invisible spirits of dead children haunting this place. *I'm going mad*, he thought. *Must be loneliness. Good thing I'm leaving.* He sat on a rock and pulled the wellingtons over his tattered socks. He was reaching for the cape when he heard them again. He crouched into foliage, looking all around. He wasn't going mad, those *were* children's voices. It was a Saturday, no school, children must be playing nearby. The fact that he hadn't spotted them yet didn't mean they were ghosts. It meant he wasn't keeping a proper lookout, which in a pilot was unforgivable. Many a flyer had gone down in flames for a momentary daydream.

There! He glanced sharply in the direction of the cry, but nothing stirred on the grassy slope. Nobody was playing King of the Castle on the rocks. *Something here*, he thought – *the shape of the terrain, a certain positioning of stones – is playing a trick with sounds, amplifying them, causing them to carry, or making them seem to come from one direction when really they are coming from another. For example, that last cry seemed to come from under the ground, which is not possible. But it means there are children* somewhere, *and so I must be careful: maybe lie low here a little longer, hope they move away.*

He was settling on his grassy bed when there came another cry, and this time he was certain it came out of the ground. He leaped up shivering, like a man who finds himself lying on a grave.

FIFTY-ONE
Feeling for a Rabbit

The foreman beckoned to his deputy. They moved a few yards from the bustle round the machines. 'Well – what d'you think?'

The deputy grimaced. 'It's like you said, Paul: we must've probed the length of the mine now, and there's no cavity.'

The foreman sighed. 'So the whole thing *did* fall in.' He gazed at the ongoing work. 'And those poor kids're under it.'

The deputy nodded. 'No doubt about it, I'm afraid, Paul. Are you going to tell the families?'

The foreman nodded. 'Got to, I suppose.

Rotten job. Done it lots of times, but never with kids.'

'D'you want *me* to . . . ?'

'No, no – thanks for offering though, Alan. I took the decision to sink that shaft, it's my responsibility. They've a right to hear it from me.'

'All right, Paul,' said the deputy. 'Do we carry on looking for . . . ?'

'Bodies, yes.' The foreman turned away, pulling out a handkerchief.

Lieutenant Ernst Pfeiffer moved tentatively among rocks and shrubbery, seeking the source of the ghostly cries. His imagination flashed a succession of bizarre explanations at his mind. *Spirits of murdered children, crying out for vengeance. A recording, designed to lure fugitives into some sort of trap. A recording designed to keep sheep away from the rocks. A concealed ventriloquist, practising.*

When he stumbled on the actual explanation, it was every bit as crazy as any he'd imagined. Between two rocks, screened by the blasted boughs and exposed roots of a stunted elder, was a crack in the ground. He noticed it only because a volley of feeble cries issued from it just as his eyes swept by.

'*Was gibt's?*' He dropped to his knees by the crack, grazing his cheek on a bough, and tried to see down it. There was only blackness. He thrust a hand in, then his arm to the elbow, to the shoulder. Fleetingly he thought how silly he'd look if somebody found him now, his cheek pressed to the ground and his arm plunged in a hole, like somebody feeling for a rabbit.

His fingers found only emptiness. He withdrew his arm and put his mouth to the crack, feeling ridiculous. '*Hello?*' he called in English, twisting his neck to put his ear where his mouth had been. Faint sounds reached him, no coherent response. He tried again. '*Hello?*'

This time a voice answered. It was weak, and unmistakably a child's. 'Help us, please.'

'Where *are* you?' called Pfeiffer. 'How deep?'

'We don't know,' wailed the unseen child. 'We can't climb out, walls too slippy. Get help, ropes and stuff.'

'How many are you?' asked the lieutenant: 'how did you get *down* there?'

'It's a *mine*,' croaked the voice. 'Walked in, another way. Four of us.'

'Are you hurt: can you not walk *out*?'

'Can't: roof gone. Please hurry, we're starved.'

Pfeiffer did not reply to this. He knelt up, brushed dirt off his clothes and looked at the crack, his mind in turmoil. *If I bring help*, he thought, *I will certainly be captured, and I am not going to be captured. I mean to return to my unit, by way of Ireland. Nothing will prevent this. Down there, trapped, are four children. They are enemy children. The Irish writer Shaw said, I have no enemies under eight. No matter. As an officer, it is my duty to escape, not to pull British brats out of holes. So.*

FIFTY-TWO

Till His Comrades Came

Mary gazed upwards. 'Is . . . is he still *there*, Gary: why doesn't he *say* something?'

Gary shook his head. 'Dunno, Mary.' He called as loudly as he could. 'Hey, mister – can you hear me? Will you help us, please?'

There was no response. 'P'raps he's gone to get someone,' croaked Tom.

Dil scoffed. 'That's what we said about Check Suit, and *he* never brought anybody.' She sat down on the clammy floor and wrapped her arms round her bruised knees.

Mary joined her. 'I'm done in,' she murmured.

'Can't stand any more of this. I thought it was over but it isn't.'

Gary looked down at the two girls. 'Don't give in,' he pleaded. 'We really *have* had it if we give in. I've got an idea.'

Dil looked up. '*What* idea?'

'Well, the shaft's not straight, is it? We can't see any sky. In fact, we can only see a few feet. If we stand on one another's shoulders, maybe we'll find the wall's not so slippery higher up. And maybe we're not as deep down as we think.'

'Yes,' growled Mary, 'and maybe there's a magic ladder, or a flight of marble stairs with thick red carpet, and a palace at the top with a banquet laid out: whole chickens, cream trifles, great big bottles of pop.' She laughed, on the edge of crying. '*Look* at us, Gary. We can hardly stand on our *feet*, let alone on somebody else's shoulders. It's Saturday up there, and we haven't eaten anything since Thursday. We're not *giving* in, boyo: we're *done* in.'

Gary sighed. 'I know, Mary, I'm the same myself. It's just . . . I don't want to die down here, and I don't know what to suggest.' He tipped back his head once more. 'If you can hear me, mister, *HELP!'*

Lieutenant Pfeiffer stuck the battered cap on his head and turned his face downhill. If he could reach those trees without being spotted, there was a chance he'd find a place to hide till nightfall. Then, walking through the night, he might easily reach the coast before morning. Might even find a boat.

He'd gone four strides when he heard the cry once more. He shook his head, gritted his teeth. *Enemy children*, he told himself. *I have no enemies under eight*, countered a little voice in his head.

He stopped, sighed heavily and turned round. Prison life might not be completely unbearable. After all, it was only till his comrades came to set him free.

FIFTY-THREE
We Do, We Do, We Do!

The foreman was trudging sadly towards his truck when he heard the deputy call. He turned. The men were gawping uphill, watching an oddly dressed figure hurrying down towards them. It wore a flapping yellow cape over a black jacket, a cloth cap, and wellingtons. *Like something escaped from a pantomime*, he thought.

The figure approached the men, shouting and pointing the way he'd come. The foreman set off back to find out what was happening. His deputy trotted to meet him.

'Paul!' Alan sounded agitated, which was

unlike him. 'Chap says he can hear kids underground, calling for help.'

'*What? Where?*' The foreman gazed at the bizarre figure. 'Is he some sort of lunatic, d'you think?'

'Don't think so, Paul. There's a uniform under that cape – German, I think. You better talk to him.'

The pair drew near to the lieutenant, who calmly watched their approach. 'Good afternoon, gentlemen,' he said as they came up to him. 'I am Lieutenant Ernst Pfeiffer of the Luftwaffe. Children are calling to me from a crack in the ground, *help*.' He shrugged. 'I cannot help, your men can, I hope.'

'Watch out, sir,' warned one of the men. 'He's got a gun.' The team came around the pilot, brandishing an assortment of heavy tools.

A contemptuous smile warped the officer's lips. 'Don't be afraid,' he told them. 'If it was my plan to shoot you, you would be dead some time already.' He tugged the pistol out of its holster and offered it to the foreman. 'Take it. I am surrendering to you for the sake of those children. Will you help them, or will we stand here *den ganzen Tag* and play at soldiers?'

The foreman stared at the pistol in his hand, then passed it to Alan. 'Show me,' he rapped, and he and the lieutenant set off up the hill, followed by all the men.

'Listen!' Dil lifted her head off her knees. 'Banging – somebody's *up* there.' She scrambled to her feet, dizzy with hunger. 'Quick – bang back.' She picked up a hunk of stone and struck the wall with it, as the other three fought to rouse themselves. Five times she hit the wall, then listened. The response came at once – five metallic chimes, evenly spaced, then a voice that said, 'Can you hear me?'

'YES!' they croaked in unison.

'Stand by,' said the echoey voice from above. 'We can't bring you out immediately, but we're preparing to send down water and food. Do you understand?'

'We understand,' screamed the ecstatic cavers. 'We do, we do, we DO!'

FIFTY-FOUR

The Sound of Coming Freedom

Richard Pritchard stepped out from behind the gorse bush. He'd been skulking there for hours with a camera, determined to get shots with a zoom lens of the children's bodies being recovered from the collapsed mine. To his delight, none of the nationals had picked up the story, which meant they'd fall over one another to pay him a king's ransom for the photos, once they knew he had them.

He'd seen the strange fellow trotting down Ling Hill and talking to the mine rescue team. He didn't *look* like a reporter from London, but you never knew: there was nothing those chaps wouldn't do to grab a juicy exclusive.

He watched as the whole team abandoned the digging and streamed over the hill behind the deranged-looking stranger. Richard was in a quandary: should he stay put, or should he follow at a distance? Surely they'd resume the search for the bodies, once they'd taken care of whatever it was the stranger was leading them to? After all, there were the bereaved parents to consider.

He decided to follow. *Must be important,* he thought, *for them to drop the job and go chasing after that chap. Might be a story in it – two exclusives in a day for Richard Pritchard, ace reporter.* He waited till the last man had crossed the skyline, then hurried uphill.

The four children gazed open-mouthed up the shaft. Something was coming down: some metallic object they could hear but not see. It kept striking the wall as it descended, causing echoey clinks. When it finally swung into view, twisting and glinting at the end of a thin rope, they recognized it as an aluminium bottle of the sort you fasten to the handlebars of your bike and fill with a glucose drink.

'*Water!*' croaked Tom. 'It'll be full of water. Who's going first?'

'*Ladies*, of course,' said Gary. 'Where were you brought up, boyo?'

'I haven't *been* brought up yet,' joked Tom. 'None of us has: that comes after the water.'

It was water, but it might as well have been nectar. They took turns, glugging the cold fluid down their parched throats. *Take sips*, the voice had cautioned. *If you gulp it, you'll make yourselves ill.* He could have saved his breath.

More water followed, then hot soup, in a vacuum flask that by some miracle survived the perilous descent. The cavers drank copiously, feeling their strength return.

When they'd had their fill and sent the empty bottles swaying and spinning back up the shaft, the voice came again.

'I want you to stand well away from the bottom of the shaft now,' it said, 'and to stay away till I tell you it's safe to return. We're going to use a machine to enlarge the mouth of the shaft so we can lift you out. You'll hear a lot of noise, and

201

debris will fall, including quite large pieces. If one of these pieces was to land on somebody's head, it would brain him. Do you understand?'

They said they did, and crawled a little way into the tunnel. Gary went last, and called out 'All right, mister – we're out of the way.'

The din that filled the chamber made them wince and press their palms over their ears, but they grinned at each other and didn't care: it was the sound of coming freedom.

FIFTY-FIVE

Live Kids is Different

Pritchard watched the activity from behind a clump of reeds. He saw a machine lugged over the hill and installed at the new site. The truck followed, driven by the chap who seemed to be boss. It was soon obvious that everybody had lost interest in what was left of the old mine.

But *why*? The odd-looking fellow who'd led them here was sitting on a stone with his head in his hands, and a man stood watching him, holding what seemed to be a pistol. The reporter saw a succession of metal containers lowered into a crack in the ground, then hauled out again. The penny dropped.

It's those kids: they've found 'em alive, haven't they? The rotten little blighters must have crawled right through the hill, just to ruin my scoop. But hey, just a minute . . .

He brightened. *Pictures of dead children make readers cry, and people enjoy a good cry. It sells papers. But a picture of children coming out alive when everybody* thought *they were dead – that'll make people feel good, won't it? And folk need something to make 'em feel good, what with this war and everything . . .* He stood up. *No need to take shots of live children from ambush. No need for the telephoto lens. Bodies, yes – matter of respect. Live kids is different. I'll talk to the boss, get his co-operation.* He set off downhill as a machine went into action, splitting the air with the hideous screech of diamond teeth cutting into stone.

He waited till the machine stopped screaming. 'Afternoon.'

The foreman looked round. 'Can I help you?'

'Press,' said Pritchard.

The foreman nodded. 'I can see that.'

'*Golfodd Gleaner*,' Pritchard told him. 'Local rag. Those kids're alive, aren't they?'

'Yes, praise be to God.'

'How did they get from . . . ?'

'Look, Mr . . . ?'

'Pritchard. Richard Pritchard.'

'Look, Mr Pritchard, these children have been buried for the best part of forty-eight hours. We need to get them out. I haven't got time to stand and chat. You can hang about, snap a picture when they come up, but if you get in the way I'll have you thrown off the site. Is that clear?'

It was.

FIFTY-SIX
There's Noble

He walked over to where the odd chap still sat, watched by the man with the pistol. It *was* a pistol, he saw, as he drew near. Pritchard introduced himself, eyeing the gun. 'Glad to know you found the kids alive,' he said, surprising himself by actually *feeling* glad. Close up, he was startled to see that the man on the stone wore German uniform.

'It was him,' said the deputy, nodding towards his prisoner. 'He heard 'em yelling and fetched us. Gave up his freedom.'

'Did he *really*?' the reporter murmured.

'There's *noble*, isn't it?' He looked at the lieutenant. 'Er . . . *guten Tag*, Herr . . . ?'

'I speak English,' said Pfeiffer.

'Oh.' Pritchard smiled. 'So do I. What *is* your name?'

'Pfeiffer,' the lieutenant replied. 'Lieutenant. Four-four-three-eight-seven-seven-nine-four-six.'

The reporter smiled, nodded. 'I know the drill, Lieutenant: name, rank, serial number, no other information. It was noble though, what you did.'

'It was also stupid,' said Pfeiffer. 'The children go home, I do not.'

'And where *is* home?'

'Hameln,' answered the lieutenant, then winced. 'Very good, Herr reporter,' he grated. 'You should do interrogating work, you have a talent for it.'

Pritchard looked flustered. 'Oh no, I didn't mean . . . it's human interest, that's all, for our readers.'

Pfeiffer nodded. 'I understand, but have nothing more to say.' He turned his head, gazed down the hillside.

Richard Pritchard wasn't too disappointed. A mean-spirited weasel, he had nevertheless

207

a poet's eye for a pretty story, and he was beginning to think he'd found one here today. It wasn't quite complete: the kids'd have to be pulled out of their hole, and he'd a few more questions, but the elements were coming together nicely. He chose a stone and sat on it, smoking a cigarette, dreaming about the job he'd soon be offered on one of the big London papers.

FIFTY-SEVEN
Who's First?

'The noise has stopped, I think.' Gary peered out of the tunnel. The light from the shaft was brighter than before. It fell on a mound of debris. As the four noticed this, the voice called to them. 'We're finished here, it's safe to come out, I'll be with you in a minute or two.'

'*With* us?' queried Tom. 'We don't want him with *us*, we want us with *him*.'

'Pipe down, you twerp,' growled his sister. 'Never satisfied, some folk.'

They crawled into the chamber and stood up. They were bone-weary and everything hurt, but they knew their ordeal was coming to an end. Indications reached them from above: voices, a shadow moving on the wall, a scrabbling noise. 'Stand clear below,' called the voice, 'I'm coming down.'

The foreman's boots dropped into view, followed by the man himself. He touched down on the mound of rubble, wearing a harness of orange webbing. He grinned at the four of them. 'I'm the voice,' he said. 'How d'you do?'

It was the happiest moment they'd ever known, but they all burst into tears. 'We're really, really happy to see you,' sobbed Dil, 'so I don't know why we're blubbing.'

'Sudden release of tension,' smiled the foreman. 'You've held yourselves together marvellously, and now you've let go. I've seen strapping great miners cry like babies for the same reason.' He unbuckled the harness and held it out to them. 'Who's first?'

Mary disappeared up the shaft, followed by Dil. Tom went third. As Gary swung blinking into daylight, the rescue team stood in a half-circle, clapping, with tears on their cheeks. Beyond them, a ragged line of people was coming over the hill. An ambulance bounced across the turf, its siren wailing. Gary wondered who it was for. The harness was stripped off him and sent down for the voice. Mary, Tom and Dil stood close together, staring dumbly at the people approaching. Gary joined them, and they surprised themselves by throwing their arms round one another and clinging together in a swaying, four-way hug.

'Question is,' murmured Gary, 'which of us is going back for the hoard?'

FIFTY-EIGHT
Natural Justice

Richard Pritchard watched the whole thing from his seat on the stone. He saw the Mossmans, the Tenbys and the Swaines reunited with the children they'd thought were dead. As they hugged and cried, he scribbled notes and snapped pictures.

He saw the people of Golfodd come streaming over Ling Hill, led by the mayor himself, to show their delight at this happy outcome. He watched the mayor thank the rescue team, how their foreman pointed to the German airman, and how everybody stood and clapped their enemy as he was led away by Sergeant Thomas and Constable Oswald.

He saw the four protesting children ordered onto stretchers and stowed inside the ambulance which lurched away, heading for the cottage hospital.

And he managed to be close enough to eavesdrop when the foreman spoke to the mayor. 'I don't know whether you appreciate how brilliantly those kids handled their situation, sir. Finding a source of water, collecting it, rationing it out: marvellous. And then following a draught till it led them to the opening it was coming from. Most people would've curled up on the floor, weeping and screaming till they died. And I mean adults. Oh, by the way, the kids told me they were forced to leave something called the Golfodd Hoard behind when the mine collapsed,' he said. 'Most precious thing in Golfodd, they reckoned. D'you want me and the men to carry on digging, try to find it?'

The mayor shook his head. 'You've just given us back the most precious thing in Golfodd,' he said. 'That hoard was buried for two thousand years: it'll come to no harm buried for another two thousand.'

The reporter's heart soared. That's it, he told himself, *the final piece of my story.*

Back in his cubbyhole at the *Golfodd Gleaner*, Richard Pritchard wrote the story that would make his name. It was the story of a town that cared so much for gold that it clung to its hoard, and was punished by almost losing its children inside a hill. That Golfodd got its young people back was thanks to an oddly-dressed man named Pfeiffer, whose name in English was *Piper*, and who came from a town called Hameln, or *Hamelin*, as it is known here. And if this story reminded readers of one heard long ago, it was probably because of a well-known poem they read at school.

The story he filed that Saturday won Richard Pritchard the job he'd always dreamed of: he became a reporter on one of the big London papers. The Blitz was on, and his first assignment was to cover one of its many small tragedies.

Two thieves had broken into a diamond dealer's home in Hatton Garden. They were in the cellar of the house when it received a direct hit from a stick of bombs. Trapped when the house collapsed on top of its cellar, they drowned as a burst water main flooded the place. Their names were Violet Weston and Neptune Lester. Their associate, Terence Bracegirdle, escaped their fate because he was in hospital after having been beaten up on Lester's orders.

Which goes to show that sometimes fate *does* serve the cause of natural justice.

Ernst Pfeiffer was freed in 1946, though not by his comrades. His home in Hameln had been destroyed by Allied bombing, and he chose to settle in England, where he became an airline pilot.

Mary, Dil, Tom and Gary never ventured underground again and yes – they lived happily ever after. Why not?

As for the coins of Carausius, they lie forgotten in the dark, like the emperor himself.